# Nanny Goat Hill

## Marie Flaim Tedford

The Tamarac Press
Underhill, Vermont
2019

Cover design by Jonathan Draudt Digital Arts
Cover illustration by Harry Crowley
Frontice and back-cover illustrations, Carolyn Bates Photography
Casual photograph of Marie Flaim Tedford, Margery Sharp

ISBN: 978-0-9907792-3-0

Published by The Tamarac Press, Underhill, Vermont
June, 2019

For readers everywhere

Maria and Annie

# Nanny Goat Hill

CONTENTS

# Preface

This collection of stories I refer to as fictional memoirs are simply germs of truth buried in the myriad jumbles that color a past.

Was there a small town like the one at the top of the Palisades, with neighborhoods of Italian, Irish, and German families? With vacant lots and fields for kids to play in, and a butcher shop and a grocery store and a cobblestone main street that seemed to go nowhere?

Of course there were.

Could these events as they spill from the pages have actually happened? Without a doubt.

It was the 1930's, a time when anything could have happened in a town that demanded stories and characters that were individual and unconventional.

Were many of these people prejudiced against people unlike themselves? They were. It was not yet a time when they questioned "the way things were," or their "Christian attitude." They speak in these stories as they spoke then.

Rascism and bigotry were not words in their vocabulary.

The storyteller's early life was a mixture of fairy tales and religion, but that doesn't mean her stories could not have happened as she tells them here. Because these stories were written at various times over several years, no chronology of time, place, or set of characters was considered, and so there are what might seem to be contradictions or inconsistencies. But each story was intended to, and does, stand on its own.

The initial motive for writing these stories was to offer a peek into a different time, culture, and life. Most of all, these are memories that could have been tucked away in a real life, and they are as real as Ray Bradbury once said of his stories in *Dandelion Wine,* "Because I say it is so."

Marie Flaim Tedford
Vermont, 2018

# Stories

# Crabs, Spaghetti Sauce, and Banana Curls

There was no sleeping that early Saturday morning. The sun kept blinking at me through a hole in the green shade and my mother's voice roared up from the dining room downstairs like a streetcar. I lay flat on my back in the iron poster bed and snapped the sheet until it swelled like a dome over my head, trying to shut out the sound of her voice.

"Whadda ya mean ya don't wanna go crabbin'? You get up outta that bed, or I'll be up there."

My mother! God! She says everything so awful. Why couldn't she talk like other kids' mothers? Muriel O'Rourke's mother would probably sound like the "Panis Angelicus" played on the organ in church on Sunday morning. So soft and sweet, it could almost make you cry.

Little drops of sweat gathered at the top of my lip and across my forehead.

"All right!" I yelled.

It wasn't that I didn't want to go crabbing. We kids waited for the crabbing season every summer, getting up early before it was too hot, then the long walk through Monument Park and alongside the dirt road that followed the trolley tracks down the side of the Palisades to the river.

If the tide was out, we ate. But if the tide was in, we would go swimming. The men went over to the rocks stuck out in the water and threw their nets in. They usually sat there smoking their pipes and talking. But my mother and my aunt did just as much work as when they were home. We had a big spaghetti dinner and then there were dishes to do and they always brought along  clothes that needed to be mended. I guess it was fun for them. We kids had a swell day.

It was good over the years, but now I didn't feel like going crabbing. I just didn't want to feel all mixed up inside and not know what I wanted. Like there were two of me.

I lay under the sheet getting hotter and hotter and thinking about what it was exactly. If I even mentioned Muriel O'Rourke and her mother, my mother would probably say, "Those Irish aren't any better than you. Ever go in their house? They hide all the dirt in the corners and under the bed where you can't see it."

My mother would never understand it wasn't just Irish or Italian, or a roof over your head, or food on the table. She would never know I dreamed of things. What would she say if I told her how I would go back in the woods and sit on the big rock by the stream and wish I could fly. Close my eyes and want to fly so bad 'til I hurt all over. The same thing she always said when she got mad at me.

"I don't know where I got you from. You're not like any of my other kids."

That always made me feel so good. Just like I belonged.

In September, I would be going to the high school. I'd be in ninth grade, and maybe I was getting too old for crabbing. That last day of school, Muriel O'Rourke says right out loud in front of a bunch of kids: "Well, Maria, I'll probably see YOU this summer, passing the house with your crabbing nets. By the way, who is that funny old man who goes with you? Is that your grandfather?"

She knew darn well he wasn't. He was a boarder who lived with us because there was a big depression in the country, and the extra money he gave my mother helped a lot. My mother could even give us a dime once in a while so we could go to the Saturday matinee at the Grant Lee.

When she made that crack, Muriel was being a drip, trying to make me feel stupid. Some of her special friends snickered and I felt all strange inside and kind of ashamed, and boy, mad.

I could hear my mother banging pots around and complaining to herself downstairs now, so I jumped out of bed and pulled on a pair of shorts and a shirt and went down to the kitchen.

My mother was filling the large pickle jar with spaghetti sauce and meatballs.

"It's about time you were up. Get me the big  pot." She never even said "Good morning," just began to list all the other things I should get.

"….cheese and bread. And don't forget to go down and get your father's wine."

If Muriel O'Rourke were going on a picnic with any of her friends, they would be taking sandwiches of baloney, liverwurst with mayonnaise and lettuce on white bread, all wrapped in wax paper. But we have to take spaghetti.

I pulled the pot out of the cabinet and put in a large loaf of Italian bread along with the cheese. My mother kept empty gallon jars under the kitchen sink, so I got one of them and went down to the wine cellar to fill it. You have to hold the jar under the wooden spigot real still, so the wine won't spill on the dirt floor. And sometimes, I put my head under the spigot and drink some. I let it trickle in my mouth, and it runs down my neck. It makes my mouth pucker and feel dry.

I heard my bratty little brothers running around the house upstairs, playing cowboys and Indians and shooting off their cap guns. When I got back to the kitchen, my mother was yelling out the back window to my aunt who lives next door.

"Adelina, are you coming? We're all ready, and we should get going before it's too hot."

Then the parade started up the street. My father and my uncle carried the crabbing nets over their shoulders. My mother and my aunt walked in back of them. Italian mothers and fathers never walk together like other people. My two brothers had on cowboy hats and guns and looked like jerks. I walked with my cousins, Katy, Nicky, Frankie, and the oldest boy, Louie. Besides all the crab nets the men carried, I was carrying the big pot. My oldest cousin carried the wine, and my mother had the jar of spaghetti sauce. Every now and then, some of it leaked out and it made a messy orange spot on the front of her dress. We must have looked real crazy, and I didn't feel so good.

We were getting close to Monument Park, and we had to pass Muriel O'Rourke's big brown house. In summer, it looked so cool. There were these big trees all around that made everything shady. Wisteria grew along the roof of the porch and hung down kind of lazy, like ripe bunches of grapes  waiting to be picked.

Muriel was probably watching  us from the porch. Maybe her mother and her fancy-dressed friends were there talking and laughing, their voices sounding like the tinkling of glasses filled with lemonade.

I would never let on to anyone, not even my cousin who was my best friend, that I was jealous of all that and wished I was a Miss Prissy. They would have laughed at me. Besides I didn't always want to be a Miss Prissy. There were times when I did things Muriel would never do, and sometimes even bad things, and I'd think about what Muriel was missing.

But I didn't want to pass that house and see Muriel smirking. She has blond hair that hangs down over her shoulders and falls into big, fat, round banana curls. And her skin is fair and sort of creamy-looking, and her eyes are blue and she wears pretty clothes that are new.

That last day of school, I could see the boys looking at her, and they had a stupid look on their faces. I felt funny next to her. I was dark, and my hair was a nothing color and cut short up to my ears, with bangs that came down to my eyebrows. It seemed like everything was so different that last day. Muriel had on a pretty blue dress and her banana curls were fatter and softer than ever, bouncing around on her shoulders like golden springs.

The boy I like best of all was following her all around the classroom, and I was watching him, wishing he would pay some attention to me. But he wasn't paying any attention to me. He was pulling on Muriel's curls and when it was time to go home, he walked out with her. I hated her and him, and it was a lousy day.

They walked down Main Street, and I walked down the other side with some creeps. Muriel and her friends and the boy I liked best in the whole world looked over at me and laughed.

I didn't know how to hurt them. All I could do was yell, "Snot noses!" And I ran all the way home and back to the woods to my rock, and I stayed there and pretended I was the only one left in the world 'til the pain went away. Whenever I thought of that day, I felt mad all over again. So, I certainly didn't want to pass the big brown house this morning, with all these bratty little brothers with cowboy hats and my mother and my aunt with bandanas around their heads and cotton dresses on. I didn't want to see Muriel's mother looking sweet and smelling like violets, or Muriel being a little pain in the neck, with her fat banana curls, looking all smooth and blonde and pretty like a blue-eyed Irish girl.

But there was the house. Muriel was alone on the porch.

I had to look twice to make sure I wasn't making a mistake. No, it was Muriel. She wore the same dress she had on the last day of school, a pale blue one with tiny colored flowers all along the hem that swirled out when she spun around and all the kids watched her and her banana curls bouncing on her shoulders. She was sitting in a rocker, just rocking back and forth. When she saw us, she waved. I turned my head and ignored her. Then she called and waved again and bounced off the rocker and came running over to us. I kept right on walking, trying to avoid her, but I noticed something, something different about her. I stopped and really looked at her.

All her blonde banana curls were gone. Her hair was cut short, up to her ears. The bouncing curls were gone. They were gone, and she wasn't pretty like I thought. Her front teeth were too big, and her nose tilted up too far—you could see right up her nostrils. And she had a long, thin face. I kept staring at her.

"Hi," she said. "Going crabbing?"

She didn't wait for me to answer. She kept right on talking.

"Did you notice anything, Maria? I got a haircut." She went spinning around on her white shoes like a ballet dancer. "Do you like it?"

She stood there with her mouth opened a little, waiting for me to say something. I could tell she wanted me to say something nice.

But I was remembering a lot of reasons why I shouldn't. The last day of school; how sad I was the day Sister Alice picked Muriel to crown the Blessed Mother during the last May procession at church; and I should have gotten the lead in the school operetta last year instead of her, and all the kids said I should have, too, because Muriel's voice had kind of a funny shake in it and sounded like she was riding over a bumpy road.

So, I really wanted to say, "You look funny! You're not pretty anymore."

I wanted to watch her face and know that I had hurt her. That I could hurt her.

But I didn't. All I said was, "Well, gee, Muriel, you can't go to high school with banana curls, can you? Besides when it grows in just a little more, it will look nice. Honest."

I just wanted to get out of there, but Muriel stopped me.

"Maria, can I come crabbing with you sometime?"

Prissy Muriel crabbing with us? I shrugged my shoulders.

"Uh, yeah, we'll see."

"Oh, what fun. Then you can come down to my house, and I'll teach you how to play tennis." She clapped her hands and bounced up and down like we had a date or something.

"Yeah," I shook my head. "Sometime. I'll call you."

Then I walked fast to catch up to my family. Before we got out of the park, I looked back real quick to see if Muriel was still there. She stood in the same spot and gave a little wave. Kind of slow and sad-like.  I waved back , not a great big friendly wave; I didn't want her to think we were going to be hanging out together. Just one of those little so-long kind of waves, 'cause maybe even Muriel sometimes dreamed things people didn't understand.

# It's a Long Way to Tipperary

Seemed like October must have borrowed some of September's sun that day. It was warm enough to run around in shorts. The air was still soft and a breeze now and then drifted by, and it's funny how sometimes it sounded like it was whispering something. Over on the oak tree near the house, a few of the leaves were beginning to let go, but most were still waiting.

Me and some of the other kids in the neighborhood were hanging around on the side of my house, walking across these narrow steel poles that connect a bunch of stone pillars my father built as a fence so no one would fall off the sidewalk and land  few feet below in a big, empty field.

The  field is mostly dirt before it fades off into weeds down by the woods. A good place to play ball or a game of under-leg, and on summer days the older boys fly model airplanes there. Lots of times the planes get stuck in the trees down in the woods that run all along the edge of the field, and we don't need a No Trespassing sign to remind us that Ann Street is on the other side of those trees.

We kids hardly ever set foot over on Ann Street, but sometimes the older boys in the neighborhood wander over to play a game of marbles with the Ann Street boys when the neighborhood guys aren't busy playing ball or they get tired of lying around in the tall grass talking about girls.

Sometimes our boys get into fights with the Ann Street boys, 'specially Sal. He's that big kid who thinks he's hot stuff, 'cause he has the best shooter when they play marbles. But mostly they only word-fight—which baseball team is better, the Yankees or the Giants, or who has the best marble shooter—and they always get around to testing each other out, see who knows more about cars, like who can tell a car just by its grill or its fenders or other stuff like that. They love cars, especially Fords and Chevies.

Well, anyway, that day my youngest brother Joey—he's ten—and this other girl—Arlene from up the road—were taking turns walking across the steel poles, and the rest of us kids were waiting to see who was going to fall off and break a leg.

Joey was doing a good job balancing himself on the pole, going very slow and not laughing, when we heard someone yell out, "Hey, kids!" It was Lucy's brother, Eddie, walking across the field toward us.

"Hey, Lucy," I said. "Your brother is coming. Do you have to go home already?"

Eddie is about fifteen, tall for his age and skinny. My mother thinks he has a tape worm.

Everybody stopped watching the tightrope artists. Joey jumped down off the pipe.

"I dunno," Lucy said. But if Eddie said she had to go home, his words were sacred, like the words in the Ten Commandments. In some Italian families like Lucy's, girls had to obey their older brothers.

"Do I have to go home?" Lucy's eyes watered up.

"No, I just want to talk to all of you about a proposition you might be interested in."

One thing about Eddie, he's probably going to grow up to be a lawyer or the mayor, 'cause he talks different from the other boys. He even sounds different, like he's twenty-five instead of fifteen.

"So what's the proposition?" I asked. I liked to read a lot, too. My favorite author was Dickens, so I knew what that word means. You can't read Dickens without knowing what proposition means.

"Well, it's like this," Eddie said. "We guys are gonna build a hut to use as a clubhouse right over there against the big oak tree."

He pointed to a tree close to the house. "Prob'ly this Saturday, and I'm the treasurer of the club, and we have to have money in the treasury, so . . ."

I was listening real good, 'cause I didn't want to miss a word when he got around to explaining his proposition. Well, it didn't take long 'til I heard him say, ". . . and if you kids sell the raffle tickets, we'll cook you a great supper in the clubhouse. We'll have hot dogs and hamburgers and beans and even a chocolate cake from Setzer's bakery. How does that sound?"

So, that was the proposition. The older boys were going to raffle off a hundred-pound bag of potatoes and we kids were going to do the work, walking around town selling tickets.

"Can we be in the club, too?" I asked.

"Of course not," Eddie said. "For one thing, you're a girl. No girls allowed. And you're too young, anyway."

The other kids were all excited about having supper in a clubhouse, but it seemed to me like those older boys thought we were too dumb to know better.

"Well, I'm not selling your old tickets just for a lousy supper you'll probably burn anyway," I said.

I waited to see what the other kids would say. None of them agreed with me. They began to clap and jump up and down like they just got invited to a party with Santa Claus, but I was beginning to feel like Madame Defarge in A Tale of Two Cities. I sure liked that book, and I figured I knew exactly how Dickens felt when he wrote about her.

"Well, I'm not doing it," I said. "I'm not doing it. So there."

"Suit yourself," Eddie said. "Be here tomorrow around this time," he told the rest of the kids. "I'll have the tickets ready for you."

He could have left it like that, but he couldn't help putting it on a little, making sure the kids didn't lose their guts or come over to my side.

"This is going to be big, you'll see. And we'll have some party."

It worked, too, 'cause if the kids had the tickets right then and there, they would have been up and down the street ringing doorbells like crazy. They probably would have rung Old Man

Peale's doorbell, even though they know the old man would sic his dog on them for setting one foot on his property.

So, that's the way it was going to be, and I just kept wondering how many tickets they would sell. Had to be enough to buy the potatoes, have some left over for the party and, heck, the boys would want at least some money just to have. I was curious to find out how it would work out, but I wasn't going to help. Not for some dumb dinner.

Eddie was right on time the next day, and he gave each of the kids, Joey, Arlene, Josie, Lucy and Melia, a book of raffle tickets. And I have to admit, Eddie did a swell job putting them together. Each book had seven raffle tickets, five cents for a single ticket, thirty cents if you bought a whole book. He must have stayed up all night cutting and stapling them together.

The kids didn't lose any time dividing up the roads between them, and I decided, what the heck, I'd just follow Lucy around and watch her do all the work.

She wasn't too bad. She didn't cry or anything if nobody answered the door or they slammed it in her face, and by the time she was finished for the day, she sold a whole book of tickets. When all the kids got together to see how they were doing, each of them sold a book. It seemed like that party was just like the gold star Sister pasted at the top of the arithmetic test paper she handed back to get you all excited about keeping up the good work, 'cause everybody was ready to ring doorbells again after school the next day.

Each day, Eddie checked on the kids and made sure they had books of tickets, and each day after school, the kids were out there going from door to door, up and down all the streets they could walk to.

And every afternoon, one of the older boys would dump a wagon full of wood pieces near the oak tree, till there were all these stacks just waiting. They never said where they got all that wood, and nobody asked. It didn't seem important.

So while the kids were out selling tickets, the older boys were busy building the hut. It's a good thing the oak tree was there and it was big, 'cause the boys decided maybe it would be a good idea to nail one side of the hut to the tree to keep their clubhouse from falling down, they said, just in case they didn't get something right. So every day after school and after supper, they were out there hammering and sawing wood. They didn't do too much measuring, they just sawed off what was left over when they reached the end of a wall on the hut.

The last job was sawing a hole in the roof for the stove pipe. Louie went up on the roof to do that and when he got finished he let out a yell, "Yay, it's done." The other boys yelled, too, and slapped each other on the back.

Time was running out to sell tickets, and Joey and Lucy each had one book left. And there was one street left: Ann Street.

None of the kids wanted to go there. It was like Ann Street had the kids all wrapped up in a net. They didn't want to run into Sal and his gang, but the kids knew they could probably sell the last two books to Mr. Lindstrom and Aunt Louisa, who lived over there, too.

They could catch the Norwegian—that's what everybody calls Mr. Lindstrom—on his way out after work. He's this short little man who always wears a train conductor's hat and overalls, and every day at 4 o'clock he comes out of his house on his way to Finnegan's Saloon, swinging a beer container. No one knows for sure if he works for a train company, but it doesn't matter. He's quiet and minds his own business, so everybody just nods hello and goodbye and that's that.

The Norwegian lives at the top of Ann Street, and down the road the kids could catch Aunt Louisa out in the garden, avoiding her two sisters who don't talk to each other. My mother says it all happened when one of the sisters, Mary, got divorced from Emil. And Honey, Mary's younger sister, got mad at Mary and said it was all her fault and took Emil's part, and then they both only talked to Louisa, and she had to give messages to Mary and Honey all the time, and it all got very mixed up. But, my mother says Louisa isn't like them. She has her two feet on the ground and knows how to handle those two. My mother always says that about people who don't laugh and have serious faces.

So, the kids decided to go over to Ann Street all together, like a gang, I guess. But none of us even wear a size 6 shoe yet, and I don't know how scared anybody in the Ann Street gang would be of a bunch of kids in shorts, but they all figured that would be safer than going alone. I went along with them even though I didn't do any of the selling, I followed them around.

Mr. Lindstrom bought the book of tickets from Lucy. Aunt Louisa didn't waste any time thinking about it and bought Joey's last book of tickets, too. We think she must have lots of money, 'cause she always puts a dollar bill in the collection basket on those Sundays when the Monsignor says, "Today will be a quiet collection." No nickels, dimes and pennies jingling around in that basket.

Joey was just putting the quarter and nickel he got from Aunt Louisa into his pants pocket, and we were going to take the short cut home through the woods, when Sal came out of his house and said, "Hey, kids, whadda ya doin'?"

We should have run, but Joey says, "We're selling raffle tickets."

"Oh, yeh?" says Sal. "Lemme see."

"Come on, Joey," I grabbed his arm and tried to get him to follow us, but Joey was so proud of selling so many tickets, he handed Sal the book of stubs.

"Potatoes, well, and who's raffling off these potatoes?" Sal asked.

"Louie and Eddie and the other big kids. They're building a clubhouse."

Sal gave Joey back the raffle book, but he didn't leave. "So, kid, how much money did you make over here?"

"Come on, Joey!" Arlene pulled on Joey's arm, but Joey wasn't paying attention to anyone but Sal.

And the next thing you know Joey was fishing in his pants pocket and showing Sal the quarter and the nickel. Before Joey knew what was happening, Sal snatched the coins and laughed.

"Well, that's thirty cents you lost, kid."

"Give it back," Joey yelled, trying to get at Sal's hand. "You're stealing."

"Get lost," Sal said and went back in his house.

Joey started to cry. "Eddie's gonna be mad, and maybe he won't let me come to the party."

Arlene made everything worse when she said, "Wait till Louie hears about this."

Louie's the oldest boy on our street, and even though he never says much and seems real quiet, nobody ever pushes him around. The kids didn't talk about it, but you could see they were all thinking about Louie. I couldn't help wondering what he would do now.

Well, he didn't waste any time and the next day after school, he and Joey went over to Ann Street. Louie said nobody but Joey could go with him. We couldn't wait till they got back. It wasn't long after, although it seemed like an hour, Louie and Joey came back through the shortcut in the woods, and Louie went into his house without saying a word.

"What happened?" one of the kids asked Joey.

"Boy!" Joey's eyes were popping out of his head. "Louie waited for Sal to come out of his house and then he said to Sal, 'Gimme back the money you stole from Joey.' Sal laughed and said he didn't steal any money from Joey, and Louie said, 'Give it back or else.'"

"What did he mean, 'or else'?" I said.

Joey is only ten and he gets pretty excited and never leaves out anything when he tells a story.

"Louie grabbed Sal by the arm . . ."

"He really grabbed Sal's arm?"

". . . and Sal says, 'Let go,' and Louie says, 'Not until I get my thirty cents you stole.' Then Sal tries to punch Louie, but Louie knocks Sal down. Sal starts to yell, but Louie reaches into Sal's pants like he thinks he'll find the thirty cents, but he didn't..."

I wished I had seen it.

". . . and then Louie pulls out Sal's shooter, his lucky shooter he wins all the marble games with." Joey stopped and looked at each one of us. "The big, red one with all the black lines running in it."

Sal never let that shooter out of his sight.

"Yeah, Joey, so what happened then?"

"And he keeps it," Joey said.

"Oh, my God, Sal's shooter. What did Sal say?"

Joey took a deep breath. "Sal said, 'Gimme back my shooter,' and Louie says, 'Not until you give me my thirty cents,' and he lets Sal stand up."

"And then…?" I asked.

"Sal called Louie…" Joey stopped and looked at us with this dumb expression, and just his mouth formed the words *son of a bitch.*

"Sal called Louie a son of a bitch? Really? He really said that. Wow!" I really wished I had been there. Even the big boys in our neighborhood didn't say that word—well, anyway, not when anybody can hear 'em.

"What did Louie say?"

"He just said, 'Yeah, and your mother wears army boots,' and we came home."

Louie says things like that.

Sal didn't come looking for Louie or making trouble, so we forgot about him after a while. Joey was happy Louie wasn't mad at him, and the kids couldn't wait for the party. A couple of days later, Lucy said that Eddie wanted only those kids who sold tickets to meet up at Mr. Martel's house—he's the superintendent of schools and lives right up the road from us—at five o'clock.

Well, I walked just as much as the other kids, so I planned on going up there with them. And anyway, Eddie doesn't own the sidewalks.

So, when we got there, Mr. Martel was standing out in front of the house with the older boys. They had all the raffle stubs in a paper bag.

"Well, now," Mr. Martel said. "Let's see what we have here." He put his hand in the bag and mixed up the stubs and then pulled one out.

"Oh, my," he said. "It's my ticket. And I didn't cheat."

Well, of course it was his. Mr. Martel bought the most tickets of anybody.

"I tell you what. Why don't I donate the bag of potatoes to your mothers? You can let them decide how to share them. Anyway, I would never use a hundred-pound bag of potatoes in a hundred years. My daughter doesn't even like to cook."

That was okay with everybody, 'cause nobody cared who won the potatoes, they were just thinking about the party.

The night of the party was on a Saturday, so nobody had to worry about homework and getting to bed early. But I was having trouble figuring out what to tell my mother when I went in to supper instead of going over to the hut with the rest of the kids.

My mother knew all about the party, but I never told her I wasn't going, so she looked at me kinda funny when I came in for supper.

"Aren't you goin' over to the hut?" she asked.

I said, "No. It's just a stupid party."

She kept looking at me and I'm not sure what she was thinking, but she never asked why. She never asks "why" to anything. To her, "why" is either a long story or a lot of excuses. She likes "no" or "yes." To my mother, they're nice steady words.

I did go out, though. I took my sweater down from the hook and slipped it on, then I sat on the cement steps across the field from the clubhouse. It was getting dark and the moon was just a sliver in the sky, and even with stars blinking away, it looked lonely. I looked at the hut, with wisps of smoke rising up out of the chimney and the smell of hot dogs frying.

The boys must have borrowed a lantern from somebody, too. Light squeezed through the cracks in the side of the clubhouse, and I could hear a Victrola playing "It's a Long Way to Tipperary." The kids were singing along, but they were having trouble with the words. Every time they came to "Picadilly," they said "Picallilly," and their voices kind of fell off.

Even though it's just a song about some Irishman who wanted to go home, the music sounded like one of those war songs, and that night it reminded me of a 4th of July parade down Main Street, all of us marching down the same cobblestone street George Washington marched on with his soldiers when he ran from the British. There are real Indians dressed in bright colors and feathers, and soldiers dressed like they just came back from the Great War, and high school bands, and Boy Scouts,  and horses, and the street is lined with people, lots of people waving flags and yelling, clapping and cheering, 'cause inside you feel like the whole world is just marching down Main Street, happy and glad it's the 4th of July, and being a country and all. I like to feel that way, but I guess sometimes it's hard to remember the 4th of July and fireworks, and that it's a special day, if you're all alone.

Well, it was too late then, but I made up my mind the next time they had a raffle, I'd do it, sell tickets or whatever.

I sat a while listening and then I went into the house. I didn't want the kids to come out and catch me sitting there alone.

After a few days, it all quieted down. The kids got over the party and Sal's shooter and all, and we went back to just playing outdoors.

We were roller skating up and down the sidewalk when Joe Murphy, the policeman who directs traffic in front of school every day, came walking down the street and walked right up to my front door and rang the bell.

My mother came to the door and they talked a few minutes, and then I could see her lips pinch together, and I knew she was mad about something. Then she invited Joe in and after a while he came out and left.

That night at the supper table, we found out what Joe was talking to my mother about: the clubhouse.

"Joey, finish your supper and then I want you to go over to Louie's house and tell him they have to take down the clubhouse and bring the wood back to Mr. Winch's lumberyard. Tomorrow, you hear? Or else they're in trouble with the cops. And no nails. They gotta take out all the nails."

The clubhouse was going to be torn down? The guys had helped themselves to the wood, and now they had to give it back.

It had to be that Sal. He's the troublemaker. He snitched to the police just because  Louie took his shooter. That's what he did.

Joey shouldn't have opened his big mouth. Now it was all over. There wouldn't be any more suppers or anything. I missed the only chance I would get. I just sat there at the table. I didn't say a word. I could hardly breathe.

I guess when I dig in my heels, my mother is right when she says, "One day, young lady, you're gonna cut off your nose to spite your face."

I got up from the table and started for the door. My mother asked me, "Where are you going?"

"Out," I said. She looked at me funny, but she didn't say anything. "Out" was another word, she liked. She knew where it was.

I ran over to the clubhouse. The door wasn't locked, so I pushed it and walked in. The room was smaller than I had imagined. I just stood there and looked around. It looked kind of nice, like somebody's house.

Not much light came in through the only window, but I could see a small woodstove over in the corner. On top of it was a kerosene lamp and a box of matches. I pumped up the lamp and lit it.

Pushed up against the wall under the window were four chairs and a table we had seen the boys bring home from the dump one late afternoon. I recognized an oak rocking chair next to the stove. It used to be on my aunt's front porch. They even had two movie posters, Tarzan of the Apes and The Dead End Kids, pinned to the wall over the kitchen table.

The tabletop Victrola that always sat in the spare room in my aunt's house was on the table, and the only two records that I ever saw with the Victrola as long as I could remember were there, too. "Making Whoopie" was on a chair, and "It's a Long Way to Tipperary" was still on the machine.

I cranked up the Victrola and lowered the arm that held the needle on the record. At first the sound was scratchy. John McCormack, he's the Irish guy singing the song, sounded like he had a sore throat. I walked over to the rocking chair and sat down. Shadows from the oil lamp jumped around on the wood boards that framed the clubhouse, and except for the music, the room was quiet.

John McCormack sang the song, same as he did that other night, same as always, like he was marching off to war. I sat back and rocked, listening for the parade.

# Nanny Goat Hill

May 4, 1935

Dear Diary,
Today is Saturday. My mother is grouchy 'cause her father is
dying. I don't know why she's crying and everything. She never
liked him anyhow. I certainly don't like him. He was mean to my
mother and my aunt Mary, that's Mama's real sister. But Mama
always says, you have to forgive. Auntie Mary just clenches her
mouth tight and she says, "I'll never forgive that son-of-a-bitch for
marrying Stepmother." Mama and Auntie Mary were just babies
when their mother died, and Grandpa married the witch, that's
what we call Step-grandmother, even though today, she's old and
tries to put on a big act like she's kind. But Mama and Auntie Mary
tell us stories about what Step-grandmother used to do to them,
and I hope she falls into a big hole and disappears forever. But
I just have to tell you this one story that Mama and Auntie told
us. One day, after Grampa had gone to work, Mama and Auntie
decided they were hungry and they were going to have something
to eat no matter what Step-grandmother said. You see, Step-
grandmother never let Mama and Auntie eat with the rest of the
family. Mama and Auntie ate the leftovers, and sometimes there
weren't too many leftovers, and Mama and Auntie went to bed
hungry. Well, this day, Mama said, they knew what they had to do.
Step-grandmother kept the key to the food cupboard on a chain

around her waist, so they knocked her down and took the key. Then they opened the cupboard and ate and ate, even while Stepgrandmother was telling them their father was going to beat them with the razor strap. Mama and Auntie didn't care. They were too hungry. Every time they tell us that story, I get all mad and I want to yell, "Give it to her good!" Grampa did beat them that night, but Mama said it didn't hurt as much, at least they weren't hungry. So, I don't know why she's acting like somebody important is dying. Anyway, she made me and my sister, Annie, clean the whole house. After we finished, my cousin came over, and we all took a bath together. What fun. There wasn't much room in the tub, my cousin is so fat. She says she needs a bra. But I have more than she does. She's just fat. Then we got dressed and went up to church to go to Confession. The "Duke," that's what we kids call Father Malloy, he thinks he's some kind of royalty or something the way he treats people, was hearing confessions today, and I hate to go to him. He's an old grouch. He yells and hollers and gives you long penances. I didn't tell him about those bad thoughts I had, though. I was too scared. I'll wait till I go to Father DeLuca, he doesn't yell. All he does is pinch your cheek and tell you to be a nice girl. Then we lit about ten candles all for a nickel. Boy, the Duke would be mad if he knew. He likes money. We didn't feel like going right home, it was a warm day, so we went back to the cemetery and peeked in those stone houses. Boy, are they spooky. We saw some kids over at the lookout tower, so we went over there, too. They were that gang of boys from Water Street. They are low Italians. We don't like them, they're dirty and they're always trying to pull your pants down. They were up in the tower and called us to come up. They were laughing funny. We hung around for a while then left. We played hide and seek outside after supper. We had fun. My mother is still grouchy.

May 5, 1935

Today is Sunday. It rained this morning, so I had to wear rubbers over my shoes to church. Me and my older sister stopped at the Kearneys to read the funnies. Mrs. Kearney doesn't mind, she left them on the porch for us. She just does that every Sunday.

She knows we'll stop in on account of my family never gets the newspaper, except Papa gets *El Progresso,* but it's in Italian and doesn't have any funnies. Mr. Kearney runs the Great Atlantic and Pacific Tea Company up on Main Street, and we shop there sometimes for Mama. My mother made homemade noodles for dinner today. They're my favorite. We pestered her to go to the movies, but she's still grouchy. We pestered her so much she gave us the money. We got the trolley at the corner. A lot of kids were going, so I got on and put the nickel in the slot and my sister and my cousin sneaked on. We do that all the time if there are a lot of people. That dumb conductor doesn't even know it. Anyway, I think sneaking on the trolley is only a venial sin, and if we get run over or something, we won't die and go to hell. The movie was good, it was a Buck Jones picture. He's my favorite. We didn't meet any boys in the movie. We got home and went to bed early.

May 6, 1935

Today is Monday and I was late for school and I had to run all the way from Fisher's field to school. You know the old house in Fisher's field has been here since the revolution. Everybody says that George Washington stayed there when he came through our town a long time ago. When I look at it, I think they are right. It's very old and rickety. Sister Bedelia made me go to the principal. She made me write five hundred times "I must not be late for school." Boy! We got our paper back in English today, and I got the highest mark for my composition, "How the Sacrifice of the Mass Is like the Sacrifice of the Cross," than anybody in the class. Even Rose Ritter the smartest kid in the class couldn't write it as good as I did. Sister said when she read it, she just wanted to sit down and say the Rosary, she felt so good. I'm going to be a writer someday. My mother gets mad when I read or write. Last week she threw the *Book of Knowledge* I had taken out of the library at the kitchen wall and the cover broke and now she has to pay for it, so she's real mad and says I can't go to the library anymore. But I am anyway, and I'll read in the bathroom where she can't see me. I stayed after school to help clean the classroom with Sister and Rita and Eddie and Donald and my sister. That Eddie is crazy. Sister got the key stuck in the cloakroom door and couldn't get it out, so she got the holy water bottle and started blessing the key. We were standing in back of her laughing like anything. Eddie says to her, "Would you like us to get the Duke?" but Sister said no and she started to cry. She cries about everything. After a while it came out. My mother was so mad 'cause we stayed after school.


May 7, 1935

Grampa died today. I don't care, I never liked him anyhow. I don't like my mother's family. You should hear them when they talk. They're so loud. I wish they wouldn't come to our house. I wish my mother didn't know them. I guess she can't help it though, 'cause Mama is a low Italian and my father's family is high Italian. He's not really my real father. My father died, but Mama married him and he treats us like we're his own kids. And he's not mean like Step-grandmother, so I call him Papa all the time. There is a lot of talking about high Italians and low Italians in our family and the street we live on, too. And I have to hear all this stuff about how high Italians are better than low Italians, and after a while I get very confused and wonder what it all means. If everybody would just stop it all I wouldn't have to be sad and worry sometimes when I don't like my mother. She was acting real low Italian today. Mama was soaking those sheets of painted scenery she gets from the old movie lot, that big glass building over on John Street, when her brother Mike came running out of the woods in back of the house. Boy I'm glad those woods are there separating us from Nanny Goat Hill where all those awful people live. I won't call him "Uncle." His face was all red, and his pants were hanging underneath his belly and he called out "Jenny, Jenny, Pa died!" Then Mama yelled. She always acts like them when they're around. Then both of them were crying and yelling and  acting just awful. I wouldn't want any of my friends to see them. I guess I'll have to go to the funeral. Anyway I'll get to ride in one of the big cars with a chauffeur. I bet none of the kids ever rode in a car with a chauffeur. I went roller skating after school with Jack. We were going around in the circle and he said he wanted to kiss me so I skated away real fast. He skated after me and I let him catch up to me and I made believe I didn't want him to kiss me but I let him, on my cheek. He likes me. His father is a vice president in a bank and he's Irish. I'm going to dream about Jack tonight.

May 8, 1935

Today is Wednesday and it is just like Spring. I only wore a sweater to school today over my uniform. Miss Devine, the school nurse, was in school today examining everybody and after she examined me she gave me a note to give to Sister. Sister called me out of the classroom and said I had to go home. I had bugs in my hair. Dorothy Farrina had to go home, too, and all the kids know she has bugs all the time, so I know they know I have cooties. I just wanted to die. What will my friends say? What will Jack think? Will he still like me? I know I got the cooties from Dorothy when Sister put us together in those double seats. I saw one bug fly out of her hair and it must have gone in mine. Mama washed my hair in kerosene. I cried like anything 'cause it stinks. I rinsed my hair six times, and put some perfumey stuff I found in the medicine chest all over it, but it still stinks. Now for sure the kids are going to know I got sent home for bugs. Jack sits right in back of me. He'll smell the kerosene for sure. My mother doesn't care, all she does is cry'just cause her father died. She says she's going to kill herself. She's acting so stupid. She never liked her father anyhow. I wish I didn't have to go to school tomorrow. But the funeral is going to be on Friday so I won't have to go to school on Friday and I'll get to ride in that big car. I hope some of the kids see me, boy they'll think we're rich. I'm not going to dream about Jack tonight. I don't know if he'll like me when he smells the kerosene.

May 9, 1935

I went to school today and the big snob Jack whispered out loud so everybody could hear, "What a smell in this classroom, smells just like kerosene." I bent my head way over the desk so it would be far away from him and I made believe I smelled it too. I looked all around to see where the smell was coming from. We had gym today and we played dodge ball so you couldn't smell my hair. Everybody was too busy trying to get away from the ball. None of the other kids said anything about my getting sent home yesterday. William Goodson wet his pants in school today and when he left the room, Sister said we shouldn't laugh at him 'cause he has kidney trouble. Mama says the whole Goodson family has consumption. They die a lot. Maybe William's kidney has consumption. It must be awful to have kidney consumption and wet your pants when you're ten years old. I don't like Jack anymore, I like Freddie now. He doesn't go to our school. He goes to the public school. He lives down the street. Tonight right after supper we played hide and seek and Freddie followed me and we hid together in back of the high hedges in Old Man Brown's yard. Everybody says to be careful of Freddie, he has hand trouble. When I ask what hand trouble means, they just laugh. I wonder if they mean he likes to touch your legs and tries to lift your dress up. He doesn't talk much, he just stares a lot and I get a funny feeling. I guess I'm in love. Tonight I'll dream about Freddie and kissing him. It feels nice. Tomorrow is the funeral so I don't have to go to school.

May 10, 1935

I don't feel so good tonight. My mother is still acting stupid. My aunt says she better stop this nonsense after all she has kids to think about. This morning I wore my yellow dress and my white hat. Me and my mother and my father and my sister took the path through the woods to Nanny Goat Hill. A lot of people were there and a lot of little kids, but I wouldn't talk to them. Then one of those fat ladies pinched my cheek and said, "God bless her, how big she's getting. She looks just like you, Jenny." And that made me mad. I don't want to look like my mother. I want to look like my father. Papa makes fun of his sisters and pretends he is one of them walking down the street, holding a make-believe pocketbook in two hands close to his chest and then he shakes his head around like a rag doll and purses his lips and says, "com-e sta?" in this high voice and we laugh. He's the only one in the family that doesn't always talk mean about low Italians. Papa says Mama's family are just as good as his family, but I don't know what to think, I get so mixed up. There were a lot of people in this big room upstairs in Grampa's house. Mama said when Grampa built the stone house, he made the upstairs into a meeting room with a stage for the band.  Grampa played the tuba in the band, and there was a place where people could dance. Aunt Josie told Mama that morning that her stepbrothers and stepsisters had a big fight last night. Some of them wanted Grampa's casket on the stage, and some wanted him on the dance floor. So I guess those who wanted Grampa on the dance floor, so he couldn't fall off the stage, won. That's where he was. Step-grandmother was there. She wore a long, black veil. She looked just like a witch. I don't like her, she always tries to give me sloppy kisses. She was crying and twisting her hands and saying all kinds of crazy things. I sat down on a chair. My great-grandmother was there, too. She's almost a hundred years old. She has only one eye. The other eye is empty and scary. She's small and all wrinkled and looks like she eats little kids. She scares me. I don't want her to touch me. I remember one time when we went to visit her and she had a basin of water and she put her hand in it and cut her arm and let some blood out. My mother said this was good. It made me sick. I wonder if she's going to live forever. She's so old. She had a long black pair of rosary beads she held in her hand and her fingers looked like skinny bones moving over each bead. Every now and then she took a small bottle out of the pocket on her skirt and drank some of the stuff in it. When I asked my mother what Great-grandmother was drinking, she said it was Holy Water. I wonder how it tastes. All the other women were crying and wringing their hands and great-grandmother just sat there and once in a while she yelled "shut up!" to the other women. I didn't like being there. The smell of flowers made me sick to my stomach and all the crying scared me. My mother was acting crazy, too. Once she gave a yell and the other women had to hold her down in the chair. They kept running over to the coffin and screaming and crying and my step-grandmother was pulling her hair out and moaning and they had to hold her down, too. I don't know why. When he was alive, all they did was fight. And call each other bad words. Pretty soon the men came in the room and closed the box. And then the women really went crazy. I just sat on my chair and didn't move. It was like being with a bunch of witches and I was scared like anything. Then we got into one of those big, funeral cars with a chauffer and that was fun. I felt so big and important. There were two little seats that pulled out on the floor. I sat on one of them facing my mother. She had a black veil pulled over her face and her eyes were closed, and she was crying. After a while, the cars started to move. Grampa's band playing slow, sad music marched in front of the cars. Grampa belonged to an Italian club and when someone died, they played at the funeral. They didn't walk very fast and it was long way to the church. The cars had to go slow, too. It got very warm in the car and I felt like throwing up, so I hung my head out one of the windows. The band played all the way to the church. It was such sad music. I cried. I wished we would hurry and get there. My stomach felt terrible. My head was dizzy and I felt sick all over. When we got to the church they brought grampa in and put him right near the altar railing. It was a Requiem Mass with more music and just when the altar boy rang the bell for the consecration, there was this loud boom and bang outside of the church that made everybody jump.

And then more booms, lots of them, one right after the other. Grampa's band was setting off a bunch of firecrackers right outside the church door. Boy! Nobody expected fireworks at a funeral. And they weren't the pretty kind, just loud booms and bangs. I never went to a funeral like this before. I was glad when it was all over. I was getting hungry. We rode home in the big car and I kept my head out the window, hoping some of my friends could see me, but we didn't see anybody, they were all in school. I'm glad the funeral is over, so my mother will stop acting so crazy. She was going to jump in the hole when they put Grandpa in, and I hung on to her dress. Maybe that's why my aunts don't like low Italians. Everything is all mixed up. I'm not going to dream about anybody tonight. I hate everybody. And I wish I was adopted so I could run away and find my real parents.

# Buck Rodgers
# and Killer Kane

Summer vacation isn't supposed to wake you up mornings worrying about things you haven't figured out yet. Summer's a time to sit under the pear tree down at the old house and think about Mello Roll ice cream cones and Saturday afternoon at the movies watching Buck Rogers tangle with Killer Kane.

That's not how it was that morning. That morning, it was worry.

It all started with string beans. Well, maybe not the string beans really, but my older sister, Annie, and my mother were sitting at the kitchen table stringing beans when I came into the kitchen after talking to Sister Matrona on the phone.

Mama and Annie's heads were bent over, and they were talking so quietly anybody'd think they were hatching something, probably how to arrange my summer vacation. No reading books. And no thinking. Especially no thinking.

My mother gets extra special nervous when I sit on our porch in the wicker rocker, thinking. Gets you into trouble, she says. She also doesn't like stringing beans, which is why Annie was there at the table helping.

When I mentioned the telephone call from Sister Matrona, Mama gave me one of those long, silent looks she gets when she suspects me of doing something I didn't do.

"Sister wants me to take these two nuns from the Mother House around town tomorrow, give them a chance to talk to the Catholics who have kids in school," I said.

The long, silent look.

"She did!" I protested. "She says the nuns want to see how the kids are doin', 'cause these nuns are the same kinda nuns we got in school. Notre Dame, that's it. They just wanna know what's goin' on. Pete's sake."

"How come Sister Matrona asked you and not one of those Irish kids?" my mother asked. Mama thinks Irish people have some kind of special powers with the priests and nuns 'cause we celebrate St. Patrick's Day, but not St. Rocco's.

"I dunno, maybe she likes me or somethin'?"

My mother might have let it go and forgotten all about it, but Annie was there listening, and she had to add her two cents.

"She's miss goody-goody two shoes, Mama, that's why. Ask her what Sister does during recess. Go ahead, make her tell you." Annie looked at me with that snide smile she uses when she really means "I double dare you."

So, I explained, very straight forward, being really careful not to make the story sound as though it were important, how this past year, Sister walked with some of us girls at recess. How she tied her long black apron around our heads like it was a veil and we pretended we were nuns, too.

I left out how I felt with the apron tucked under my chin and covering my hair. How I felt special. My mother would have yelled, "You are not going into any convent, do you hear me, young lady? Get those ideas outta your head."

Mama was convinced that nuns and priests weren't normal.

"I told you, Mama," Annie taunted. "I was right. So there."

"You shut your mouth," I yelled at Annie. "You're just a big shit."

"Nice," my mother said. "Nice words to call your sister. What would the good sisters of Notre Dame say if they heard you, huh? What would they say?"

I didn't want to argue. I just wanted to figure out how to get the nuns to all the Catholic houses before 2 o'clock, so I wouldn't be late for the movies.

"Maria, I'm asking you, not anyone else in seventh grade," Sister had said on the phone. "I know you're dependable and how you want to be helpful to us here at the convent."

But this was the start of my summer vacation, I wanted to tell Sister, and I had important things to do, like get to the Saturday matinee at the Lee Theater to see if Buck Rogers was going to escape the amnesia helmet and remember who he was.

But instead, I told her I would chaperone the two nuns around and maybe, I thought, I could save time and skip over some of the Catholics no one thought were important, like the old Italian lady who didn't speak English. Nobody saw her all week, anyway, except on Sundays when she attended Mass. And she dropped a nickel in the collection basket on the first Sunday of the month when no one else in church dared drop in anything but a dollar bill. Especially after Monsignor Murphy stood on the altar steps with his bushy eyebrows sticking out from his forehead, his face all red and puffy, saying in his Irish brogue, "Today will be a silent collection."

Then he'd lower his head and peer over his glasses as though he dared anyone to disagree with him before he walked down the aisle with the collection basket.

But now, instead of figuring out how to get back home in time for the movie, I had to worry about my mother and my sister ganging up on me.

Sometimes I did make up stories about joining the convent and just being holy for the rest of my life. So what if I thought things like that? So what! I didn't always think holy things, but I certainly wasn't going to tell anybody the other stuff that went on in my head.

The next morning, I was at the convent at 10 o'clock. The visiting nuns of Notre Dame were waiting on the closed-in porch. Sister Cordelia was tall and pointed-looking, like the silhouette of a beanpole, and Sister Mulvena, the other one, was short, and round, with a red, splotchy face.

"Good morning, Sisters" I said, feeling very special and very holy. They smiled, and Sister Mulvena said, "So you're the young lady who is going to show us around town."

"Yes," I said, "I know all the Catholic families in the north end of town."

"That is so very nice of you to give up your Saturday to come with us."

Well, if Sister wanted to think I was a nice girl, I guessed it was OK, like it wasn't a sin or anything if I really didn't want to be there.

I walked in front of the two nuns, and every now and then, I would point out something I thought was important, like the Riley's place. The old house always looked dark even with the sun shining on it. The house sat way back off the road, and in front of the building on a small patch of lawn, a flaking statue of Garibaldi tipped a little but managed to keep from falling over. What helped keep the statue up were at least three or four Harley Davidson motorcycles always leaning against it.

The house was dark brown with a dark brown porch that circled around it. And no matter what time of day, there were always men dressed in jeans and leather jackets sitting out there, drinking beer.

"And in that house," I said, and I kind of talked a little quieter, trying to sound like I knew what I was talking about, 'cause this was very grown up stuff, ". . . that's where the Riley girls live, and Monsignor Murphy excommunicated them last year."

There was a slight gasp.

"Young lady," Sister Cordelia said. "Are you sure you aren't repeating gossip?"

"I was there," I said and turned to look at the good sisters. "It was at the 11 o'clock Mass, and the Riley girls were in the back pew, and they wore pants and had on leather jackets, and when Monsignor Murphy was swinging the incense ball around blessing everybody during Benediction, he said right out loud that those young ladies in the back row were not allowed in church anymore dressed in pants and that they were not allowed to ride motorcycles with those men, and they were excommunicated until they learned how to act like Catholic ladies."

I nodded my head up and down to emphasize what I was saying. I wanted the good sisters to know that it wasn't gossip but the God's honest truth. Sister Cordelia wasn't happy with the story.

"Young lady, I think we have had enough of that. I'm not sure you aren't just exaggerating a little. Why I never heard such a tale, and I'm sure the Monsignor did no such thing."

Well, he did, and I decided if she wanted to be that way, then Sister would miss some other good stories I could tell her about other Catholics. We walked on in silence.

The first few houses we stopped at, Sister Cordelia did the talking. She asked about the family, how many children, how old, what grade were they in school, how did they like the school, did they go to church on Sunday. That kind of stuff.

The women seemed real glad to answer the questions and had a few questions of their own. Like, why were the nuns coming around and asking questions?

Sister Mulvena put in her two cents and said they were taking a census of Catholic families to see how the schools were working, were they doing a good job with the children. The women smiled politely and didn't seem to want to talk anymore about it, satisfied with her explanation.

We finally got to the last of the families, the Dornans. Theirs was the last house before the road to the cemetery, and it sat up on a knoll. The house seemed to fit right next to a cemetery. The dark brown shingles were worn and faded, and the shades drawn over the windows made the house look as though it were empty, and I thought, lonesome all by itself.

A flight of cement steps with grass growing through the cracks led up to the front door. Sister Mulvena walked up slowly and was a little out of breath when she got to the top, so she leaned against the house while Sister Cordelia rang the doorbell. But they both almost fell against me when the door opened, and we were all splashed in the face with water.

Mr. Dornan stood in the doorway with his wife. She was holding a small bottle of holy water with a cross embossed on it.

The Sisters wiped their faces and looked at each other, but they said nothing.

Mr. and Mrs. Dornan invited us in just like it was normal to throw holy water at people.

The room we walked into was dark, with heavy green shades

pulled down over the windows. When I got the holy water off my face, I looked around and noticed a miniature altar that resembled the altar at church only it was small enough to sit on a table in a corner of the room. It had a lace covering, and small candlesticks with candles flickering in them.

I was beginning to feel funny, like I was at one of those scary movies. I could tell that Sister Mulvena and Sister Cordelia were thinking about the altar and everything, too. They turned to each other and their eyebrows were raised, and their eyes looked like they were asking each other a question. But they still hadn't said a word.

Then from somewhere in the house, but it was hard to tell from where without more light, this tiny woman dressed in a long black skirt and a gray sweater scurried into the room. She walked hunched over. Her hair, kind of a mixture of gray and white, stuck out from her head like the thin branches on a pussy-willow tree. Some of it fell into her face and covered one eye. A pair of rosary beads dangled from her hand and swung back and forth as she circled the room.

She slowly eased over to Sister Mulvena and looked her in the face, real close. Sister stepped back, and the woman came over and looked at me. Then she walked around the room again, round and round in a circle, clutching the beads.

She gave each one of us a long stare as though she were studying us to see if we were in the right place or what should be her next move.

Finally, Mr. Dornan said, "Aunt Rachael, we have guests, so you must sit down and be quiet." Mrs. Dornan took Aunt Rachael by the arm and led her to a chair. Then she invited the Sisters to come closer to the altar. Wasn't it lovely and what did they think?

By then Aunt Rachael had left the chair again, and she scurried like a mouse over to the altar. She stood very still, only her head moved every now and again to look back over her shoulder at the rest of us in the room.

Before anyone could stop her, she threw herself down on the floor and stretched out her body and her arms until she looked like a cross lying there. I could see Sister Mulvena's face in the dim light. She looked like I felt when I saw Bela Lugosi sink his teeth into his victim's throat in that movie Mark of the Vampire. I had wanted to close my eyes, but I didn't want to miss anything, either.

I couldn't take my eyes off Aunt Rachael. Then I felt Sister Mulvena's fingers gripping my shoulder. Sister was scared. But Sister Cordelia just stood there, pursing her lips and scowling as though Aunt Rachael were one of her naughty students.

Mr. Dornan just shook his head back and forth and Mrs. Dornan knelt down on one knee alongside Aunt Rachael and talked sweet and soft like she was singing "O Salutaris Hostia" at Benediction.

"There, there, Rachael, everything is fine," she said. "We're all safe, and Jesus loves you. Now get up, Rachael. The good sisters will be leaving, and we must thank them for visiting."

Aunt Rachael wasn't getting up for anybody. Mrs. Dornan explained to the Sisters that Aunt Rachael sometimes got a little emotional. She'd be all right after we left.

But you could see Sister Cordelia didn't want to hang around and talk about it anymore.

"Of course. We understand. These things happen. We'll leave now, and I'm sure everything will calm down. Thank you, and may God bless you."

Boy, Sister Cordelia was really brave. You could tell that she was probably the kind of nun who wouldn't have covered her eyes at the Passion Play when the thunder rolled and the stage went dark and the soldier stuck his spear into Jesus. She probably would have just sat there until the lights went back on and said, "Well, that was a very nice play," and then made sure all the kids got back in the bus and nobody got lost.

As we walked out of the darkened house, I felt as though we had been in another world. Even Buck Rogers would have scratched his head.

The good sisters spoke very little on the way back to the convent, only once in a while reminding me to watch for cars crossing the main street. I had to turn around and check every so often to see if they were still with me.

When we got back to the convent, I stood at the foot of the steps not knowing what to say. Sister Cordelia stood very straight and bossy-looking, stared right at me without a smile or anything, and said, "Thank you, young lady," and just walked into the convent.

I was about to turn and leave when Sister Mulvena, hanging back a little, stopped me and said in a whisper, "Now Maria, what you saw today, the Dornans and their house and everything..." She stammered. "...Poor Aunt Rachael...well, you mustn't think about it again, ever again, do you hear me? Just put it out of your mind."

She was bending over me so close she could have poked me in the eye with her nose. I just shook my head up and down, yes, yes, yes, like I was a puppet and somebody was pulling my strings.

And then Sister Mulvena said, very slowly, as though each word could make something bad happen, "If you think about Aunt Rachael, and the altar, and the holy water, and what happened, and try to figure it out...," she closed her eyes as though she couldn't look at what she was thinking. When she opened her eyes again, she said, "...it could drive you crazy."

I didn't understand what Sister meant. But especially, I didn't understand why Sister looked so sad and a little afraid, too.

I didn't say anything, just turned and ran as fast as I could down Main Street, across Jane Street, then over to Center Street, and into the house.

My mother was stirring soup in a large pot on the stove. She looked up when I came in.

"What's the matter with you? You look like the devil is after you." She had that half smile on her face, expecting me to tell her about the day, but I wasn't going to tell her anything, not anything about what happened at the Dornans, and especially not what Sister Mulvena whispered.

I was having trouble getting sister's words out of my head. They were like a bunch of bees buzzing inside my brain. And it didn't matter at all what Buck Rogers and Killer Kane were going to do that afternoon when the lights went low in the theater and the kids clapped and stamped their feet when the MGM lion roared on the screen, throwing his head from one side to the other.

Mostly, I could only see Sister Mulvena standing at the bottom of the Convent stairs sounding as though she had been talking to herself, warning herself to forget that day and everything that happened. And when she said that stuff about "going crazy," the words scared me as much as the dark room with Aunt Rachael holding onto her rosary beads, scurrying around as though she were looking for something she'd lost.

# The Change Purse

I don't know if my memories of the last time I saw my father are in the exact order they happened. Sometimes I wonder. Are memories events that really occurred, true, pristine, scene for scene? Or are they mere fragments we select from myriad brain cells, stitching them together to make a life, as we do pieces of material to make a quilt—selecting colors that look good together, designs that give drama.

But this is what I remember.

Palm Sunday. Strong arms lift me out of the bed and carry me down the hall past the room where my father sits in his bed, propped up against the pillows, looking wan and thin. He is ill. Consumption, or what we today call tuberculosis.

The strong arms that lifted me belong to my cousin, Primo, and he stops.

Yes, I know he stopped.

After all these years I can still peer into the room and see my father waving ever so slowly as I am carried past the room and out to the waiting car. I have pneumonia and my mother, already burdened with a dying husband, a new baby, and two other children to care for, cannot take proper care of me. So I am being sent to my aunt's house until I am well. This morning I weave in and out of consciousness and only vaguely remember the short ride.

When I awake again, is it the next day? Days later? The fever is gone. The room is dark. The shades have been drawn on all the windows. I am in my aunt and uncle's bed room. I recognize the bed I am lying on, a soft feather mattress that puffs up like a balloon. My cousin Melia and I use it as a trampoline on rainy days.

It doesn't take long for my vision to accustom itself to the dark, and I am surprised to see in another bed alongside mine, Melia, staring at me. Even in the shadows, I can see that her face is covered with spots. She has measles.

Melia is two years younger than I am, and her older sisters and brothers spoil her. She is sitting upright in bed and sticking her tongue out at me.

I am too sick to care. I cannot remember anything about that moment other than her little, red tongue pointed in my direction.

I was confined to my aunt's house for over a week, and snapshots of time continue to pop into memory. But what feelings passed through me during those days I cannot remember, as though I were only there in the shadows. My mother did not visit, or surely I would have known the plump, blonde-haired woman with watery gray eyes had slipped through the shadows to claim her presence there.

There are other visitors, uncles, aunts, neighbors, smiling, bending over me, murmuring, "Poor Maria, poor little thing," slipping pennies and nickels into my hand, as if those solid, valuable coins could somehow reassure me that all was well.

The coins are spread out on the table beside the bed.

But there is more to the whispers and sad looks and the coins slipped into my small hand than I know at first.

The days pass, and by Easter Sunday, Melia's spots disappear and she is in and out of bed. The green shades are raised from the windows and sun pours into the room. My aunt tries to give the holiday some meaning. She brings me a chocolate bunny and jelly beans and puts them on the table alongside my bed.

Relatives make their way up the stairs to see me and Melia,

filling my hands with coins that I put with the others. But the pennies and nickels keep falling on the floor and under the bed and slipping in between the sheets and blankets. So my aunt gives me a small leather change purse to hold them, and it slowly fills out like a mouse stuffing himself with cheese.

While I was awake I didn't let the purse out of my sight. I don't remember if it was the next day or two days later, or when, but another cousin, a girl, stood at the foot of my bed, small, short-haired, with a mouth pursed into a pout. I know she came from across an ocean with her father and mother and older brother, and that she was a cousin, but we had not yet gotten to know each other. After more time passed, we became step-sisters.

My cousin is about eight years old and speaks English, but slowly.

"Your papa is dead," she says, looking at me as though she were telling me that it is raining outside.

"He is not!" I raise my voice, and I am afraid.

"Yes, he is. I saw him in the box," she says. And I scream, "Zia, Zia!"

My cousin's lips tremble.

My aunt is there. "What's the matter?" she cries.

"She says Papa is dead." And I point to my cousin, by now fear welling in her eyes.

"No, no," Zia says. "No, he went on a trip, a long trip on the ocean. That's all. Just on a trip."

But I know she is telling a story.

My aunt grabs my cousin by the back of her dress.

"Bad girl," she says, and drags her out of the room.

He was dead. He was gone. My father. I would never put polkas on the phonograph for him again, so he could dance on rainy Sunday afternoons. We wouldn't take summer afternoon rides in the Model A car out to the airport to watch the planes take off, or buy honey and farm-grown ears of corn along the way.

He was gone. My mother was alone, and he wouldn't be there

to take her in his arms and show her how to smile, how to enjoy the day out with her family.

I hug the small change purse. The leather feels so soft and smooth. Over and over, my fingers trace the sides swelling with coins. I will offer it to my mother, of course, when I see her again and she will feel safe as I do when I hold the purse close to me. She will be happy I gave it to her.

Days pass and Primo is there again and I am dressed and taken out to the car for the short ride home. As we pull into our driveway, the backyard is awash in brilliant sunlight.

And here, if only I could thread my own image of that morning into a memory, my mother would be smiling with outstretched arms and I would be safe again.

But I do remember that morning more clearly than any other memory of that time.

I step out of the car and see my mother, dressed in black, a black shirt and a long black skirt, her hair pulled back into a bun at the back of her neck. She is scrubbing the wooden stoop. She stops when she sees me and clasps her hands together in front of her. She stands, waiting.

Her face is quiet, but there is no smile to welcome me home. I walk over to her very slowly. I wait. She says nothing. I hold out my hand and offer her the fat little change purse. She reaches out and accepts it. Then I watch her hand clutching the purse slide slowly down the side of her skirt and disappear into the deep folds of her pocket.

# The Afternoon the Cicadas Sang

Something terrible happened that Sunday afternoon. Nobody can tell me different. Not that anybody ever does: they just don't talk about it.

It was one of those hot days with a special look Sunday gets late in August—you know, like it was dressed up and had to be taken care of, not get any spots on it. Everything stopped and got quiet, except for the sound of the bells ringing up in the old stone church on Hill Street, echoing from one end of town to the next for each of the Sunday Masses. The stores closed, of course, but the bakery and the soda fountain over on Main Street stayed open 'til four o'clock. My mother put on a corset and a clean, starched dress and a ruffled apron that she had trouble tying around her waist. And instead of whooping up a game of Marbles or Johnny-Ride-the-Pony out in the open field, we kids hallowed the day and went for walks after Sunday dinner instead, all dressed up like we were going to church.

Now, they're all acting like that afternoon was just any other day.

But David's limp body the men had carried into my aunt's house was real and so was the white Packard convertible in my aunt's driveway where David had parked it earlier that Sunday afternoon.

Just after Sunday dinner, this car had pulled into my Aunt's driveway with a bunch of men and their wives, laughing and talking in Italian or broken English, wherever they could find the right word. David, was driving. They'd come over on the ferry from New York City and were looking forward to spending Sunday afternoon drinking and playing bocci under the grape arbor in my aunt's backyard. The men played bocci, anyway. The women always got together somewhere away from them, so they could sew and gossip.

When I ask about David now, my mother acts like she's suddenly deaf or I wasn't there in plain sight asking a question. And when I ask about the old man—he was there, too—my mother says he's where he belongs, where he can be taken care of and it's none of my business, anyway.

Well, I don't think she should say that, 'cause I'll tell you why. Ever since I can remember, the old man boarded with us. Well, you could say he really lived in the basement where he had a table, a chair right next to the furnace, and a small bedroom with a bathroom next to the wine cellar.

Mostly what I remember are shadows and sounds, and sometimes I don't know who is who or where the sounds came from. But I do remember the old man, just like a picture of him shuffling through my early years in heavy work boots was glued in my head. He was old. I don't ever remember him young. He had gray, curly hair that grew long in back and disappeared into the collar of his flannel shirt. He never left the house or the yard except once or twice a year he'd go hunting for rabbits, and maybe he'd come down to the river and go crabbing on a summer day with the family. Mostly, he just stayed around the house and never talked to anybody. But you could hear him cursing every now and then under his breath—"son of a bitch"—if he walked into the woodpile right outside the cellar door when he was drunk, or just because he felt like it, or something happened no one else knew anything about but him.

I don't remember when he started it, but maybe once every winter he'd take all us kids down to the local Hofbrau for ginger ale and pretzels. Boy, he was something on those days. No dirty old overalls. A clean shirt. A coat. You wouldn't have recognized him from the old man who rattled around in the dark basement.

He never invited us kids to come along, but he'd let my mother know he was going and she would just say, "The old man is going down to Cella's this afternoon. Dress warm." And then we just watched every step he made, and when he went into his bedroom, we followed him. He was going to open the yellow trunk we were told never to touch. Looking into the papered trunk, that was something special all by itself. As soon as he opened the lid, a smell filled up the room like it was hiding in the trunk just waiting to get out. It was a smell that wasn't anywhere else in the house. It was like it came from somewhere far away, some unknown place, like in the fairy tales, magic. Everything was magic, after that, his only pair of dress shoes, black, shiny leather shoes with these deep creases locked in just like the wrinkles in his face; his hat, not a cloth hat like my father's, but black and smooth and when you touched it, it felt like fur; a white shirt he wore with his overalls; and the long, black coat with a big fur collar that made him look like he was a king or something. We kids would walk ahead of him down the road, skipping and jumping like we were those jesters you see in old storybooks.

He kept other things in the trunk, too, large pieces of paper with strange words and pictures on them that he brought over to this country. German money. "By and by," he'd say, not to anybody, just out loud more like he was talking to himself, he'd be rich someday with all that money. I heard my father tell him once that he should throw it out, it would never be good again, but the old man left the money just where it was. At the bottom of the trunk were photographs he never let us see, especially the one in a yellowed, brittle envelope with some writing scrawled on it that I couldn't read. If any of us kids tried to reach into the trunk to get at the pictures or the envelope, he'd reach out with an old hairy arm and grab whoever's hand was in the trunk and yell, "NO!"

You could see his whole body go stiff and his eyes would change. Most of the time they were old and watery looking, but when he stiffened, there was a meanness in them. His whole face changed, and he got mean looking. He wouldn't say another word. He didn't have to. No one wanted to see what his meanness would do.

He didn't have any friends. He hardly ever spoke, except to his dog or to himself when he sat winter nights in the basement getting drunk, so drunk my mother would have to run down and check the furnace 'cause he kept shoveling in coal like he had to empty the coal bin in one night.

The thermometer gauge would be hopping and jumping like it was going to blow up, and my mother would shout, "Are you trying to burn the house down? Look at you. No wonder no woman wants you. Who would want a man who does nothing but drink and eats nothing but pork chops and never says a word like he has no tongue?"

She could have screamed all night. He didn't seem to hear her. He just looked at her with blank eyes and said nothing.

Well, anyway, one day before that Sunday afternoon, I got to thinking about all those pictures the old man wouldn't let us see, scattered over the bottom of that trunk, tumbled around waiting for somebody to pick them up and look at them. Waiting for me.

Maybe it was because summer was fading. Maybe it was because the cicadas were buzzing, real loud it seemed like, and the grapes hanging on the vines in the backyard were turning purple, and you could almost smell them if you stood under them and closed your eyes. Maybe it was one of those days when everything, inside and outside, seemed like it stepped out of a fairy tale and could disappear before your eyes at any time.

Anyway, I checked first to see where the old man was. He was sitting on the woodpile outside the cellar door, fast asleep with a bottle of wine at his feet. I figured he'd be there for a long time. My mother and my aunt were sitting under the grape arbor in my aunt's backyard, talking. They probably had a lot to gossip about. So I went next door to my cousin Millie's house to see if she wanted to explore the trunk.

"Nah!" she said. "Pamela and me are going to sew doll clothes under the pear tree down at the old house, and we're bringing cookies and having a tea party. Wanna come?"

Any other time, that would have been swell, but not that day. That day I wanted to see those pictures with faces of people I never met, who were dressed in clothes that were different and didn't look like anybody I had ever seen. Like they came from another world. And I especially wanted to see what was in the envelope.

"Suit yourself," I said. I was annoyed. "And I'm not going to tell you what I find, so there. And anyway, I hate sewing doll clothes. Your mother is always telling me my stitches are too big. Who cares, anyway?"

I stomped out and I hoped she'd stick herself with a needle and have to put peroxide on it and it burned.

No one was in the basement, so I went into the bedroom. The trunk was pretty big and somebody a long time ago had painted it yellow. The old man never locked it. I knelt down and lifted the lid. The photographs were at the bottom. I reached in, pushing aside the old money and clothes, trying to find the envelope with the words written on it that I couldn't read.

I picked up a handful of pictures. I wondered why there were men dressed like the grandfather in that book, "Heidi," with short pants and funny hats and smoking long-stemmed pipes, but most of the women didn't look too different from my mother. When I opened the envelope, there was just one picture: two men and a pretty girl dressed in a long skirt, her hair pulled back off her face. She was standing between the men and all their arms were linked together. The girl was laughing and looking up at one of the men, a light haired young man, almost like a boy, who looked down at her smiling. The other man was watching them, but he wasn't smiling. His face was serious, even a little angry. I looked at the photograph carefully. The angry one looked like the old man might have looked when he was young.

I knelt there staring at the picture wondering what was going on, and I didn't hear the old man open the door and come into the room. But I could see him walking toward me out of the corner of my eye, and I was just about to drop the photograph back into the trunk when he grabbed it out of my hand. He looked down at me, his eyes full of anger and meanness.

"What are you doing? Who told you you could go in my trunk? You have no right. . . ."

I stood up, frightened. He raised his hand and his fist was closed and he was going to hit me when my mother came into the room and yelled.

"That's enough. I'll take care of her."

She grabbed me by the arm and took me upstairs, and I knew she was mad.

"What did I tell you? Do you listen?" She sat me down at the table and her face was red. It wouldn't have mattered any if I told her about how I felt, why the trunk was so exciting.

"But, Mama . . ."

She wouldn't let me explain.

"I don't want to hear your excuses, you hear me? Just stay away from that old man's trunk."

But I couldn't just let it go. Why did the old man change into some kind of a monster when he saw the picture I was looking at? My mother had no intention of telling me anything else, so I sat there and didn't say another word, trying to understand what happened.

After that day, the old man was different. He kept to himself a lot. When we did see him, he said nothing. He looked especially mean when he saw me, so I made sure I didn't have to see him at all.

On that Sunday when this man David, who I never saw before, and the crowd from New York City came to my aunt's house, the old man sat most of the morning on the front steps drinking. When the white Packard pulled into my aunt's driveway, the old man didn't move. He sat and watched them.

They were noisy, talking a mile a minute in Italian. The women were busy straightening out their dresses after the long drive and examining their hair in the car's rear view mirror.

As soon as David stepped out of the car, you could see he was different. He didn't act like any of the other men. He was quiet. He talked, but not as loud as the others, and when he talked to the women, he spoke very low, almost in a whisper. He dressed different from the other men, too. I never saw my father or any of my uncles dressed in a white suit like the one David wore. Even his shoes were white. But it was his hair; bright red with shiny waves that looked as though he used a curling iron. You couldn't stop looking.

I couldn't wait till after Sunday dinner to see him again, to watch him in his white suit and red hair.

Later, after dinner, my father joined the men under the grape arbor to play bocci. I walked over to where the ladies had gathered under a cherry tree in my aunt's yard to sew and talk. David sat with them.

I watched every move he made. I had never seen anyone like him, except maybe in the movies. First he'd sit with one of the women; then he'd sit with another; and every time, he put his arm around their shoulders and bent his head down close to their face. The women were having a good time.

No one noticed me. I sat on the grass where I could see what was going on, but didn't get in the way. From under the grape arbor, there was a lot of noise, someone played an accordion, and the men were singing songs from the old country. Bocci balls clashed against each other and the cicadas' buzzing seemed to hang low and louder than ever.

I pulled out blades of grass just to keep busy when I noticed the old man slowly walking toward David and the women. He looked like he was walking in a daze, like he was sleepwalking or something. Just very slowly, he walked toward them. They never noticed him.

Then he was standing right in back of David, who was whispering in one of the women's ears. The old man's arm reached around to the back of his overalls, and from one of the deep pockets, he slowly pulled out a hammer and raised his arm up over his head. And then, I saw it come down and disappear into David's red hair.

A spurt of blood ran through the waves and trickled down on David's white jacket. His head slumped over and fell on the woman's shoulder. She was screaming and by this time so were all the others. One by one, the men came running over to where the old man stood like a statue. He never moved. The hammer was still in his hand. I never moved. I just watched and wished the cicadas would stop, just for a minute.

"Jesus Christ! What did you do?"

My father grabbed the hammer and put it in the old man's pocket. Two of the other men carried David's limp body into the house, while the women cried.

"Stupido, stupido!" my father said over and over, as he and one of those guys from New York led the old man back to the house.

I went back to the house, too, and stayed there for the rest of the day trying to understand. And I couldn't help thinking about the photograph.

My mother and father put the old man to bed. He never said a word; he didn't cry or talk about it, he just got into bed and did what my father told him to do. Just like a baby.

The next day, the old man didn't get out of bed, and I heard my mother tell my father that it was time to do what they should have done a long time ago.

"Should have put him away in the old country," my mother said. "Sending him to America didn't help."

She got on the telephone and called somebody. I heard her say she would have him ready. Later in the day, a car came to the house, and they put the old man in and it drove away.

That was the last time my mother ever said anything about him.

I guess hitting David wasn't the first time the old man didn't know what he was doing. My mother and father went on about stuff, talking mostly in Italian and once in a while I understood some words, like "young girl" and " the old man was acting crazy," but I could just tell by the look on my mother's face she was glad he was gone.

Nobody ever talked about that day again. My father cleaned out the old man's room and used it to store tools and stuff. They took the trunk to the dump. My mother didn't even open it. I wanted to take out some of the pictures, but my mother wouldn't listen. All she kept saying was, "Mind your own business. How many times did I tell you to stay away from that trunk? You never listen, 'cause you're a busybody."

By the time my mother and father finished cleaning out the

basement, nobody would ever know the old man had lived there. Nobody would know that one Sunday afternoon a man dressed in white drove a long Packard convertible into my aunt's driveway, either. Some men had come and taken the car away.

I think about that day, seeing the hammer over David's head falling into that wavy red hair, the red blood streaming down his white jacket.

Maybe I should have just left the photograph on the bottom of the yellow trunk where the old man had buried it.

# The Easter Hat

Jenny watched a fine spray of dust dance in slow motion along a slice of sunlight cutting across the oak surface of her dining room table. She ran her hand over the table's oiled surface, examined her palm for dust, and wiped it on her apron.

"Anna! Maria! Are you coming down?" she called out. "You're going to be late for church. Did you hear me, Anna?"

She leaned against the bannister at the foot of the stairs and shifted the weight of her solid figure to one leg while she waited to hear the sound of bureau drawers opening and banging shut.

"I heard you, Mama. We'll be right down."

Satisfied the girls were up, Jenny went back to the kitchen to finish the noodles she was preparing for Easter Sunday dinner. She slapped a swollen ball of dough onto a wooden breadboard, sprinkled it with flour and began to knead, but she couldn't help thinking back to her own childhood. Sunday was like any other day for her. Could she have been just ten years old, Maria's age, when she would rise with the sun and walk a mile to milk one of the goats in their fenced in field and carry the milk back for her half-brother and half-sister's breakfast?

She shrugged her shoulders.

Jenny could never bring herself to get excited over the holidays. There were no memories of chocolate bunnies, spring outfits, and frilly bonnets. She thought of her two daughters. Anna, so strong, so grown up. If Jenny could have expressed herself, she would have described Anna as being sturdy as a wooden spoon.

And Maria! There was a tremor in Jenny's hands as she shaped the ball of dough, remembering Maria's childish chatter the day before.

"Easter Sunday is my most favorite in the whole year, Mama." Maria had waited as she always did for her mother's response, but Jenny turned away from the upturned face begging to share the mysteries of involvement. Maria continued to talk on and on.

"I have the whole day planned," she said. "And I'm going to wear my yellow taffeta dress, my new white sandals, and my tan onion skin hat. I'm going to look very special, Mama, won't I?"

Jenny was deep in thought remembering that moment when Anna walked into the kitchen

"Morning, Mama," she said and kissed her mother on the cheek. "Happy Easter."

"Happy Easter to you, Annie," Jenny said. "Is your sister ready or is she going to make you late for church? If she isn't down in five minutes, you go without her. Maybe one of these days she'll stop her dreaming."

Anna watched her mother roll out the dough.

"Whenever I ask her a question, she never answers me. She says she's busy thinking," Anna said. "I might as well not have a sister, Mama."

"Thinking about what?" Jenny asked. She worked the dough, stretching it out over the board, wider and wider.

"I don't know," Anna said. "This morning when she woke up, she spent ten minutes just watching the sun come up over Old Man Brown's house. That's why she isn't ready."

Jenny slapped the dough, rocking her entire body. Anna backed away from the table to keep the flour from spattering onto her blue silk dress.

"Mama," she asked. "Where's my navy -blue straw hat? Is it in your closet?"

"Yes, but wait a minute before you go upsetting things," Jenny said. She wiped her hands on her apron and led Anna into the bedroom. From the top shelf of her closet she brought down a large brown paper bag and shook out several hats onto her bed.

"Here," she said, holding up the blue straw trimmed with a navy-blue bow pinned to its wide band. "Here's yours. Try it on. We should have done this last week."

Anna stood in front of the mirror on her mother's dresser and put the hat on.

"I think you're right, Mama. I should have tried it on last week."

Jenny frowned. "It's too small. Now what are you going to wear?"

"Maybe Maria's will fit me," Anna said. "She can wear mine. After all, I'm older and bigger."

Jenny hesitated. "Maria will be so mad."

Yesterday, Maria had babbled on and on. Most of what she said, Jenny heard only as a background of sound. Lent and purple sadness. Words. Words. But Jenny clearly remembered "My tan onion skin hat with the brown tassel goes so well with my yellow taffeta dress, Mama."

Ever since Maria was a baby, there was a strangeness between mother and daughter that Jenny could not understand. She knew only her impatience whenever a melody or lilt came into Maria's voice, as they so often did.

Jenny looked over the hats. "I don't know what to do." She shook her head, inhaling and exhaling loudly. "I don't know why you didn't try it on before this. You're old enough. When I was your age, I was selling violets at the ferry."

Jenny remembered the wicker basket she used to carry flowers in when she was a little girl. She'd pick only the longest-stemmed, deepest purple violets to gather together and tie with string. Then she'd walk down to the ferry slip and set herself down where she could engage travelers going to and from New York City.

"Violets?" she would ask shyly as the crowds swept past her. From some, there came polite smiles, at times a coin was pressed into her small hand and a bouquet was admired and carried off. At the end of the day, she would throw the wilted flowers that were left into the dark river where shallow waves lapped up the violets and carried them bobbing out to sea. Watching them disappear made her sad. Then she would remember why she was there, reaching into her pocket to feel for the coins she would bring home.

Maria's voice from the upstairs bedroom erased the shadowy memory.

"Alleluia! Alleluia!" she chanted.

Jenny grabbed the onion skin hat with the tassel. "You kids don't know what it's really like."

"I don't know why you're so worried about Maria getting mad," Anna said.

"All right! All right! Wear it. If she gets mad...well, she should have been down here by now. Let her get mad. A hat isn't important."

Anna quickly adjusted the hat on her head and left, while Jenny went back to the kitchen, mumbling. "I don't know where Maria gets her ideas from. Not from me." Jenny was certain of that. She carried the large breadboard over to the kitchen sink and scrubbed it until the wood looked like it had been bleached clean. Food on the table. A home. No one can kick you out. That's what mattered.

"Morning, Mama," Maria entered the kitchen and kissed her mother noisily. "Isn't it a beautiful day for Easter?" Maria never noticed the set of her mother's mouth. Instead, her gaze darted from the strands of noodles carefully laid out on a white cloth and over to the bread pudding waiting on the stove.

"Oh, it's just perfect! With apples!" she said.

"You're going to be late," Jenny scolded.

"Annie go already?" Maria asked.

"If she waited for you, she'd be late, too. Now hurry up. Get a hat and go to church."

Jenny did not look at Maria, but she sensed the small, bird-like face, the dark eyes bright with anticipation. She waited as Maria went to the bedroom.

"Mama, where's my hat?"

Jenny did not answer.

"Mama?" Maria called again.

"I gave it to your sister to wear."

"Mama!" Maria's voice cracked. Jenny went quickly to the room. Maria stood on a chair, one arm stretched over her head, searching the closet shelf.

"Come down! I said I gave it to your sister."

Jenny picked up the navy-blue straw hat.

"You can wear hers. Here. There's no good reason to get upset."

"But, I don't want to wear that hat. I want mine. Why did you give it to Annie?"

"Your sister's hat was too small for her. Yours fit her just right. What's all the fuss about?" Jenny pushed the blue hat down over Maria's head while Maria watched her image in the mirror.

"It doesn't fit me, either, Mama," she said. "Look. Look how it sticks up. It looks like a soup pot on my head." Maria began to cry. Jenny turned away.

"I never had an Easter hat. Sometimes, I didn't have shoes," she said.

"Mama, please," Maria begged, as Jenny pushed and pulled the hat down over Maria's short black hair. Each time she released her hold, the straw yielded back to its own form and the hat sat there like an inverted bird's nest.

"It looks all right," Jenny said. Why, just this once, couldn't Maria be like Anna.

"But this is Easter, Mama, and everything is supposed to be special and right. My hat matched my dress and made me look nice. I look like a dope in this hat."

"Nobody's going to look at your hat." Jenny raised her voice. "Now, go to church."

"I can't wear it!" Maria sniffed and wiped at her face.

"Stop crying," Jenny shouted. She snatched the hat from Maria's head and began to stuff it back into the bag. "All right. Stay home."

"But, Mama . . . I can't . . . It will be a mortal sin, and if I die before I go to Confession, I'll go to hell, Mama."

"You're not going to hell. You're going to church. Now take this hat and go to church." Jenny offered her the hat again.

Maria stared through her tears at her mother's face and the extended hand clutching the straw hat. She grabbed the hat and ran from the room. Jenny heard the front door slam. Slowly, she moved to the window, parted the lace curtains, and watched Maria kicking pebbles in the dirt road as she shuffled toward Main Street and church.

For a moment, Jenny stared at the disappearing figure. Angrily, she brushed her hand over her face.

# The Bracelet

$E$arly one morning, on her way through the small kitchen, Christina tripped over a Seth Thomas clock sticking out just far enough from under the kitchen table to send her slapping against the cast iron sink.

Christina was a large woman who not only carried an expansive waist and an ample bosom, very often making it difficult to bend, but she had to walk cautiously as her swollen ankles circling her legs like huge doughnuts made it impossible at times for her to see where she was stepping.

She screamed but didn't move, just leaned against the sink. When she did finally turn to face Jack, there was more than pain clenching her lips and squinting her eyes.

"That's it, Jack. Are you listening to me, Jack? I coulda killed myself. I've had enough of these clocks all over my kitchen."

She waved her arms around, pointing to the sink, the table, the windowsill.

"This time it's for good. I'm leaving. Do you hear me Jack? I'm going to Minnesota to stay with Catherine."

Jack sat at the kitchen table, his head bent over the innards of another old clock. He looked up but as usual said nothing. He should have warned her, he knew that, given some explanation, told her he had stuffed the clock under the table, just for a while, until he could get around to figuring out why it was running so fast. But Jack was a quiet man, frugal with words. Over the years, he had also learned that one word to say he was sorry and Christina would drag up 25 years of living with a man who never talked, whose only hobby was fixing clocks. A man who had driven Catherine out of the house, his only daughter, with his silence.

Christina lost no time putting together one small suitcase and another bag with a few personal items, some photos, and her favorite cup and saucer. Using one of Jack's canes, she retrieved a Chase and Sanborn coffee can from under the bed. It was filled with bills and some coins she had been saving, along with a gold ring that could no longer slide down over her knuckle. She carefully wrapped the money and the ring in one of Jack's socks and tucked them into her purse.

Jack was still at the table when Christina came to the doorway and announced she had called for a cab and was leaving.

"Now you're going?" he asked.

"Now," she said, "Not another minute, not another day, Jack, you hear me?"

"Catherine know you're coming?"

"For years, Catherine knows I'm coming. For years. She won't be surprised. Florence Palermo, up on Nanny Goat Hill, she'll be surprised. All Nanny Goat Hill will be surprised. But not Catherine."

Jack shook his head. "The way you talk, sometimes, Christina."

But Jack knew his wife was right: Nanny Goat Hill would be surprised. The close-knit families that lived in that small section of town where he had been born had welcomed Jack and Christina's marriage with more than joy, with relief. Jack would have a common-sense woman to love him and take care of him. She would accept his habits, his willful estrangement from people, his taciturn nature that prompted most people to avoid him. But the intrusion of clocks wherever you looked in the small bungalow began to try even Christina's patience and only reminded her of Jack's silence as the years went by.

Jack knew it was useless trying to convince her to stay now. She was a stubborn woman. Nothing would be gained except angry words passing between them. So he said nothing. She'll stay awhile with Catherine and then she'll be back, he convinced himself.

He followed her out to the front yard of the small bungalow where they lived all these years and watched as she got in the cab and it disappeared up the road.

He stood there thinking pretty much the same way he thought all his life. Whatever happens, happens. There isn't anything you can do about it. All the talking in the world was just that, talking. And he wasn't about to change at this time in his life. There was the horse and the chickens to feed, there was his job picking up junk and metal if he wanted to eat, and there were his clocks to be mended, to set to telling the right time.

When the breakup made the rounds of the neighborhood, it gave people something to talk about.

"I don't know how she lived with that man all these years," summed up how the women felt, though they were not fully sympathetic to Christina. They couldn't defend a woman leaving her husband. No, it was not right. After all, it was against the church. And didn't all the women in the neighborhood have troubles, a husband who beat his wife, another who drank too much? So, no, it was not right.

The men, of course, saw it differently, lamenting how hard it was living with a woman who nagged all day, day after day, needed a good slap . . .

Jack, never one to consider the goings-on in the neighborhood, went about his daily routine as a rag picker. Each morning he hitched the old workhorse to the wagon and set out collecting rags, junk, tinfoil, scrap metal, and whatever else would bring him a buck. He came by a lot of his clocks this way.

Jack was just a young man barely out of his teens when he fell into the rag-picking and scrap-metal business. He had always been shy and tongue-tied when it came to talking to people. But the business suited him. His customers on the road expected nothing from him except an offer to buy their discards. No words. No friendship. No amenities.

All in all, he had done well and could afford to buy the house where he and Christina had lived for a short time when they first married. The building sat awkwardly, to the back of the property—a tall, angular stone house with a long row of steps that looked like a ladder leading up to the front door.

From the first day they were married, she begged him to build a bungalow near the front of the property. A little bungalow, she said, where they could be closer to the road, that was not so hard to clean and had "a normal staircase" to the kitchen door. Something easier to climb with her short legs.

The stone house, she said, was not a home.

"Look at it," she would remind Jack every day, "It's a strange building. Why would anybody build a house like that?"

She called it the skinny house. "Look at how narrow they made that house and so tall with all those steps to climb to get to the kitchen door."

Jack gave in and the stone house turned into a repository for the extra things he picked up: tools, a statue of Garibaldi, legless chairs, a World War I gas mask, rifles, and bureaus that needed drawers, not to mention boxes of small things, broken dishes, odd cups, horse bridles, and anything that looked as though he could make it functional. In time, entering the house by the front door became a hazard.

As the years went by, Jack added two goats to the backyard. Christina complained. What prompted her frequent outbursts of anger were the clocks that had multiplied in the kitchen and, in time, all over the house. He had developed a hobby of repairing the clocks, the only thing Jack did outside of his job as a rag picker.

Alone again, Jack resumed his daily routine, discovered new routes to new customers and he stopped waiting for Christina to tire of Minnesota.

The years slipped by and Christina settled in with her daughter's family, occasionally dropping Jack a line to see how he was doing, but carefully avoiding any talk or hope of a reunion.

One day Jack's neighbors noticed a woman's bright red skirt and a flowered shirt on his clothesline. It didn't take long for news to get around the neighborhood that Jack was living with a "nigga woman," or maybe one of those "mulattas."

"Is she black?" the women in the neighborhood asked.

"No, you know, half-and-half," explained Mr. Mecurio. "Name's Mary." He had seen the woman up close one day when he passed the house on his way to borrow some tools from DeAngelo at the top of Jack's hill. Jack and his woman were sitting on the front porch. Mr. Mecurio nodded his head.

"Afternoon," he said, and paused briefly, just long enough to check out Jack's woman. Jack had nodded, and Mary returned his stare. As he was leaving, he heard Jack call her name, "Mary."

The talk didn't last long. The neighborhood, mostly Italians and Germans, had a Depression to worry about and rotten kids that resisted family rules, always in scrapes with the police or each other, intent on growing up fast and independent. They didn't need to worry about Jack and his woman.

They settled back into their everyday routine, trying to keep a roof over their heads and followed their own law, live and let live.

So Jack's woman became part of the world they lived in. Like they did with the other common-law wife in the neighborhood, Lena Dick, the neighborhood had their own way of dealing with an unwed couple, perhaps the easiest and least complicated way. Simply call the women by their first name and add the man they live with for identification and let it go at that. So, Mary just became Mary Jack, Jack's woman.

For a while the neighborhood women watched Jack's house for the comin's and goin's, expecting heaven only knows what, but they soon tired of it and forgot about Mary and tended to their own business.

Some mornings Mary and Jack hitched up the horse to their wagon and did not return home till the sun had begun to set behind the hill across the road from the bungalow. They'd come back, the wagon weighted with bags of rags and all manner of junk.

Other mornings, Mary rose early and gardened, putting in long rows of vegetables and roping it off from the goats. The neighbors could hear her singing.

"And I ain't got weary yet, and I ain't got weary yet."

And on the clothesline, always, flowered skirts and bright shirts.

As the days and the years went by, Mary's hair, which she kept pulled back from her forehead and gathered into a knot at the back of her head, started to gray under the bright red bandanas she wrapped around her forehead. She wore large, round earrings and rings on all her fingers. On those afternoons when she did not accompany Jack, she would sit on the front porch and rock. And soon Mary would start humming. And maybe she'd sing a few lines of a song, or maybe she'd just hum and rock until it was time to start supper

One day, mending a pair of Jack's pants, Mary ran out of thread.

"Jack, I need some thread, some black, brown, and maybe some more red thread," she said.

Jack nodded his head up and down, which Mary had learned meant he agreed. "Tomorrow," he said.

The next day, Mary said she would like to walk to the Five-and-Ten-Cent store, look in some of the other stores on the way. So she and Jack leisurely walked the mile down to the Five-and-Ten-Cent store in the center of town.

The store was quiet, with just one other customer. The proprietor, a red-faced man who was a member of the synagogue in town smiled. "Can I help you?" he said, somewhat uncomfortable when he noticed Mary. Still, it was none of his business; he was there to sell not to question.

"I need some thread," Mary said and walked toward the counter where spools of thread were spread out neatly in boxes. "I want some black, some brown, and some red thread."

The proprietor smiled again. "Well, pick out what you need. I have the best selection in town."

Jack stood behind Mary and didn't say a word. He just watched her roll the spools over and over in her hand, examining the size, the color and the price. She looked at Jack.

"What do you think?"

Jack shook his head. "You know."

Mary took three large spools of thread and handed them to the proprietor. "Anything else I can help you with today? Slippers, towels, some lipstick?"

Mary shook her head and began to walk down the aisle, touching the articles on the counter until she came to the jewelry—

boxes of rings, and earrings, and pins. And on a wooden frame, bracelets. Bright, colorful, dangling bracelets.

She stopped with a slight gasp. She picked up a bracelet, a set of simulated gold rings that were held three-together and slipped it on her arm and smiled when the rings jangled together with just a soft metal sound.

Jack watched her.

He turned to the proprietor and pointed to the bracelet on Mary's arm along with the threads and paid for them. Mary did not take the bracelet off, she just walked out of the store shaking her wrist this way and that. She smiled all the way home.

From that day, Mary wore the bracelet day and night. In time, the simulated finish dimmed and Mary's hair beneath the scarf turned white. Jack sold the horse, the wagon, and the goats, and all the clocks but the gingerbread on the kitchen mantel. He took more and more to just rummaging through the junk he had stored in the stone house. One day he emptied out the house and put the years of collecting on the street with a sign, "Free." Most of it was carried off, and what was left, he stored in the barn.

Then he rented the house out to a young man who didn't mind walking up twenty-four steps to the kitchen door.

One afternoon when he was done puttering around in the barn, Jack walked up to the porch where Mary rocked each afternoon. The rocking chair was still, and Mary sat there with her eyes closed. Jack poked her.

"Mary" he said. But Mary did not answer him, and Jack listened for her breathing. He sat there for a while and then walked over to the neighbors to use their phone to call the undertaker. He had long since had the phone removed from the bungalow as an unnecessary expense. The neighbors were sorry, they truly were, for they had accepted Mary, even though they just passed the time of day with her, nothing more, no visiting, no cups of coffee.

Then Jack went back to Mary on the porch and carefully removed the bracelet from her arm before the undertaker came to get her. He dropped the bracelet into a flowered cup and put it on a shelf in the kitchen over the sink next to the gingerbread clock.

After that, Jack just wandered around the place, spending his afternoons sitting on the porch. He was surprised the day a letter came from Christina.

"Jack, I am coming back to Nanny Goat Hill. Florence Palermo said she would drive me down to see you. She says you're alone now. We could talk, anyway, Jack. We're both getting old, we need somebody . . ."

Christina came with Florence a few days later, and Jack said nothing, just nodded his head. They went into the house and right off Christina noticed that the clocks were gone.

"OH," she said, "the place looks nice, Jack. Just like a little cottage. Some new curtains. . . ." She picked up one of the panels on the kitchen window and examined it on both sides. "They don't cost much." She turned and faced Jack.

"Well, what do you think? A few years maybe we have."

Jack shrugged his shoulders. "If you think so."

Christina moved back that week and immediately began to clean. She started in the kitchen. In a corner of the room, she set a large garbage can and, as she moved around the room, began to fill it with what she considered junk. Jack said nothing, but as he watched her rearranging furniture, dusting off things, her face frowning, and the sound of her voice complaining like a stuck record on the Victrola, he could not help thinking how little Christina had changed. A little slower getting around, but there was the same feeling he had. How little he had known about her in the beginning.

She began to dust the shelf over the sink, took down the flowered cup and dumped the bracelet out in her hand. Cristina wasn't expecting a piece of faded jewelry. For a moment she held the aging bracelet and then just as quickly she threw it into the garbage.

"You can take this out and dump it in the barrel in the backyard," she said.

Jack said nothing and carried the can out to the back where he had a large tin barrel he used as an incinerator. The day was quiet, and the sun was setting behind the hill. Jack looked around at the empty stable where the horse had been and the stone house now in need of paint, the twenty-four steps to the front door cracked and falling apart, the weed-infested garden where Mary had grown vegetables and where he had buried her ashes after the cremation. He began to dump the garbage into the barrel, slowly, carefully, until he caught the bracelet.

He blew off some coffee grounds that had stuck to it, then he wiped it on his pants trying to bring back some of the shine.

He stared down at the trinket and his eyes watered as he tried to grab the words he had always kept to himself, that always seemed to tease him, that would be there even through his silence.

So much he should have said but he'd kept to himself. He remembered the day Mary put the bracelet on her wrist. He wanted to tell her then, what? What was it he wanted to tell her? How beautiful it looked, how beautiful she was, how happy he was? Could he have told Mary how he felt? He should have tried, but Jack shook his head. The words would have stuck somewhere then, too.

Off in the distance he heard Christina call. Carefully, he folded the bracelet, slipped it into his vest pocket and walked back to the house.

# Snake in the Grass

Ididn't know Millie before Emil Heil divorced her and spread rumors around that Millie "wasn't performing her wifely duties," or something strange like that. Whenever the ladies sitting under the rose trellis sewing on summer days mentioned Millie and the divorce, they giggled and laughed. Sounded to me when I was close by listening, they never gave Millie a chance to tell her side of the story. They just pushed her out of their lives, too. I guess Millie must have felt the world wasn't the same for her anymore and she had to figure out how to make it work.

Maybe Millie knew it and maybe she didn't, but she just had to know she was never going to be that Millie again, the Millie she was when she first married Emil. According to the ladies under the rose trellis, they used to treat Millie like she was Mrs. Astor's pet horse. She made the neighborhood look up and take notice when she visited, dressed to kill in those fancy silk dresses, fur coats, and high heels that tapped on the sidewalk like keys on a piano. When she stopped by for a visit and they served coffee, there were no heavy diner cups on the table. The women set out special china cups, "Made in Japan," on white tablecloths, and cookies from the Great Atlantic and Pacific Tea Company.

Now, all that's forgotten and Millie's just the old lady who passes the house every day wearing a cotton dress and a bulky, dark-blue sweater with small holes in the sleeves, like she forgot to change her clothes to go out in public. Her skin is real white and looks almost like chalk against her dyed black hair that she pulls back into a bun. But nobody would notice her and she'd fade into the morning, except when she gets as far as our driveway, she stops and looks all around, as though she suddenly doesn't know where she is and she's looking for something familiar, something to tell her where to go. The fingers on one hand fold over the other hand that holds her sweater closed tight against her, and her fingertips tap, tap, tap, impatient, with nails painted so bright red she could stop traffic on Main Street.

It seems like it's a good thing her feet know where she's going. She turns into our driveway, overgrown with grass since we don't have a car, and walks down to the dirt path that runs under the grape arbor and then weaves past the chicken coop ending right at the end of our property. That's where it meets the fence around the old homestead— Millie's family homestead, where she spends her day.

That's what started Millie's trouble with her sister Honey, Millie going down to the old homestead to spend her days after Emil left. Everybody knew Emil settled a lot of money on her and gave Millie their house after the divorce. And Millie got him to promise never to set foot in town again as long as he lived. Or no divorce, not ever. Everybody knew Emil had a girlfriend he wanted to marry, so Millie got her way.

But that didn't mean Millie didn't get lonely and want some company. Like she says, since the old homestead was left to her two sisters and herself, she was entitled to enjoy her inheritance while she was still alive, spending her days there along with her sisters, Louisa and Honey, and their husbands.

But Honey had other ideas. You have to understand about those sisters. Louisa was quiet and no matter what happened, the Depression, infantile paralysis, somebody died, Louisa would just say, "It's God's will." So Millie coming down every day was just another one of those things she had no control over. Honey, I guess, didn't care what God had to say. She could talk for herself.

"You just can't walk in here and think this is your house like you did before you got married," Honey yelled. She talked loud all the time anyway, so raising her voice didn't bother anybody, 'cept, of course, the neighbors knew all her business whether she wanted them to or not.

"This is my house as well as yours," Millie said.

Honey just yelled louder, and you would have thought she was falling off a cliff or something.

"No, this is not your house. Louisa and me pay all the expenses. You don't. And I'm not paying for you to stay here. You have a perfectly good house. And why didn't you be a good wife. Emil was a good man. You think you're gonna get another man to take care of you? Ha! Well, think again, dear sister."

Well, I guess Millie did think again, but she still had something to say.

"Emil was a son of a bitch! A liar and a snake in the grass. You didn't live with him. I did. And all I want now is to come down and have some company. All you hadda do was ask me for the money. I could pay my way. So, I'm coming down and you can't stop me, unless you want to throw me out."

That was the last time Millie and Honey talked to each other. Millie kept right on coming down to the homestead, bringing her own food and leaving at the end of the day. If either one of them wanted the other to know something, they went through Louisa, used her like a puppet to deliver the message. After a while, Louisa didn't even have to be in the room. She could have gone down to the store to pick up a loaf of bread or gone out to the garden to pick some parsley, and Millie and Honey would keep talking to each other as though Louisa was still in the room.

"Tell her I'm having an icebox installed on Friday," Millie might say.

"Tell her we need another icebox in this small kitchen like the cat needs two heads," Honey would answer, just as though they didn't know Louisa wasn't there.

So that's how it was after Emil left Millie.

You know, sometimes it's hard to figure out how you get to know people. Know all about them—their name, what they do, and where they come from and everything. One day they're just there and then, like it's a long time later, you're friends. But you can't remember what happened in between.

That's the way it was with me and Millie. One day she said, "Hello, there, you must be Jenny's little girl." Well, I was nine years old and I didn't think I was a little girl, but I said, "Yes." And then I can't remember what happened after that, but when I saw Millie, we had lots of things to talk about, and it's just like I'd known Millie since, I don't know, forever maybe.

Sometimes I like to talk to a grownup. Not my mother, or my aunt who lives in the stone house next door to us. The only time they talk to me is when they want me to do something like go to the store, or hang out the wash, or something boring like that. But, Millie, she just talked to me, about anything, about the wind that might be blowing leaves around and filling up the gutters, or the "poor little rabbits" my father keeps for Sunday dinner in those screened-in boxes near the garden. We could talk about anything, and I didn't even have to stand still. She'd talk to me even if she had to yell 'cause I was disappearing up the cherry tree in front of the house.

She especially liked to tell me about her "adventures"—those are the times she leaves the neighborhood to go shopping or just go somewhere. Well, one day Millie must have thought she discovered O'Reilly's Funeral Home on Main Street where it's been stuck between the jewelry store and the bank for as long as I can remember. She got so excited. According to her, she'd just gone down Main Street to shop, that's all, like she does every now and again, but for some reason—maybe the way the sun's shadows looked that late afternoon on the large glass storefront—she said she stopped and looked real hard at the building.

"Well," she went on shifting from one foot to the other and twisting a handkerchief in her hand, "I got to thinking about it and I thought, you know, I never saw a body go in and I never saw a body come out of this place. Not once. Mmmm. I thought again. Is this a place for dead people? Mmm."

Millie's eyes get real big when she's excited about something, and her mouth closes over her teeth, and her lips gather together like a prune.

"Did you ever think about that when you go by O'Reilly's?"

No. I never think about dead people or O'Reilly's, but I didn't tell her that or she'd feel bad, so I went along. And she told me she thinks it's not a funeral home, but a secret place for those Black Hand gangsters who live down on Water Street.

I don't think so, but I liked the idea anyway. Gangsters are a lot more fun than dead people.

And then there are times when Millie just teased me about boyfriends and wanted to know how I'm doing in school with "those nuns." Just like my mother, Millie doesn't like nuns.

Millie didn't say mean things about people like some of the women in the neighborhood, but she did look angry when she talked about how handy it is to have a man around the house if something goes wrong, and then she called Emil "that German bastard who ruined my life."

"That's what he is," she said, "a snake in the grass." I know she felt bad acting like that, though, 'cause she quickly drew in her breath in a big "Ooooooooooo," and looked at me with this scared look and her eyes wide.

"I just said a bad word. Don't you tell your mother, or she won't let me talk to you anymore." She put her finger up to her lips.

"Oh, my mother won't say anything," I told her. "She calls Monsignor Murphy that all the time."

Millie just seems to walk through the neighborhood these days like somebody who shouldn't be here. People treat her like she should be on one of those islands with those poor lepers Sister Bedelia is always talking about. Just somewhere else, 'cause nobody's her friend anymore. They just think she's strange, and they run when they see her coming.

If Millie feels bad, she doesn't say anything to me. She just goes about her way, which I don't always understand, but I can't help thinking about some of her odd rituals, and I know the other ladies think about them, too.

Like when she leaves her house any time of day, but mostly in the morning. Around 11 o'clock she walks out the side door, locks it, and then walks to the end of her driveway. Then, just like someone comes from somewhere and taps her on the shoulder, she stops and looks back. She stares at the house as though it might have disappeared. Well, you could say that's not too odd, but she does that little ritual all the way to where the road starts downhill—walk, stop, look back—until she can't see her house anymore.

But if you listen to the other ladies in the neighborhood—and I try to, 'cause you can hear lots of good stories when you do—they still talk about Millie, but mostly about Emil. Men always seem to be the good guys, like the cowboys in the western movies. He was a plumber, he had a good business, and he was a good provider. A good provider! Boy you should hear them. They talk about him like he's one of the apostles who fed all the people who came to hear Jesus talk about stuff. They talk a lot about husbands. Beats me.

One fall day, the air was just starting to give you duck bumps if you didn't have a sweater on. Millie stopped by when my cousin and some other kids were playing potsy on the sidewalk in front of my house.

"Hey, you kids, how would you like to make some money to go to the movies on Saturday?"

"Yeh, Millie! Whadda we have to do?" I asked.

"Well, I been thinkin' it's about time I cleaned up around the house. I might want to sell it one of these days and go live at the old homestead."

We all knew Honey and Millie didn't talk, but we figured Millie knew what she was doing.

Anyway, she wanted us to rake and stuff. Pull out the weeds and clean up the place a little. And the best part, she said she would give us all 25 cents each. That would get us into two movies with enough left over for a box of jujubes.

"Come over to the house tomorrow after supper," Millie said. "and we'll build a bonfire and roast some marshmallows, too. How does that sound?"

We were there the next afternoon ready to work. Millie was pulling out weeds near the front porch that must have been real nice once for sitting out on a summer night, well, before part of the roof caved in, anyway. It wasn't just the porch, the shingles were fading into different shades of green and here and there, big pieces were missing. When we checked out around the outside of the house, we couldn't tell a flower bush from a weed. Millie said to pull it all out, she was never going to plant a flower or an onion ever again. Boy, it was a mess. But we were excited, especially about the bonfire and the marshmallow roast.

Millie opened the doors to the garage, a wooden building that looked like it was built at an angle. When we went in, she started naming off all the things that belonged to Emil—a shovel, a rake, some old car parts and other stuff. She started right in.

"I hate that wheelbarrow; it's Emil's." Or, "That dumb hammer was Emil's favorite. I should have hit him with it."

We got kind of confused. Every time we went to get something, she hated it 'cause it was Emil's, and we thought we shouldn't touch it. She must have guessed we didn't know what to do, which wouldn't have been hard, 'cause we just stood around looking stupid.

"OK. Take the wheelbarrow and the rakes. Go on, take 'em. Take 'em, I don't care."

For the next couple of hours, we pulled weeds from around the foundation and out of the driveway and filled the wheelbarrow and listened to Millie work herself up like a clock spring ready to snap.

"Damn that Kraut. Look what he left me."

I never saw Millie like that before. It was like she was remembering things she thought she had put away somewhere and forgotten. I didn't understand, hard as I tried.

I tried to think about the Millie I knew, and after a while, I didn't listen to her anymore. I just pulled out weeds and cut down overgrown shrubs like the other kids. We took turns pushing the wheelbarrow across the street and dumping the rubbish on the edge of the road near an old falling-down fence.

It was starting to get dark when Millie decided the brush was high enough for the bonfire, so we sat on the fence to watch her get it started.

Millie rolled up a piece of newspaper, lit the end of it, and held it to the rubbish. The fire started slowly and then it flared up and you could feel the heat. The dry weeds crackled and shriveled as the flames swept up and scattered sparks all around. Millie had a rake in her hand and was pushing back at the weeds that slipped out of the pile.

Suddenly, my cousin Melia shouted, "Hey, Millie, it's a snake. There it is, it's wriggling out of the fire. See it there on the ground?"

A small garden snake crawled out from under the burning brush and slithered toward the edge of the road.

Millie let out a whoop and started hopping on one foot and then the other as though she were dancing. You could see, she was excited, like there was something she had to do. She swung the rake out and brought it down hard, pinning the snake on one of the prongs. It kept on twisting and squirming trying to get free, but it was caught tight.

"I got 'im! I got 'im! He's dead!" Millie shouted.

Then Millie carried the snake, still wriggling, over to the bonfire and shook him off into the flames. And all the time, she was smiling. She smiled even when we heard this crackling sound like something breaking up, and then a loud puff when we think the snake must have exploded and sparks flew out all over.

We kids didn't say a word. Maybe it was the snake blowing up and all, or maybe we all felt as though we had lost Millie, the Millie we knew anyway. So, I don't think any of us was thinking about roasting marshmallows. Even the 25 cents Millie said she'd give us for the Saturday matinee didn't feel good anymore.

And Millie—we couldn't tell what she was thinking right then, or if she even remembered us or where she was.

Way off down the road, I could hear my mother calling. I jumped down off the fence and the other kids followed. There wasn't any reason for any of us to hang around anymore. We took our time, though, walking slow, like if we didn't Millie might think we were deserting her. None of us was feeling much like whoopee! and home free! and all that stuff.

Half way down the road, I turned to see what she was doing. She was still standing there, leaning on the rake, real quiet, staring out across the fence and the dark creeping through the oak trees. She wasn't fidgeting or anything like usual; she wasn't even smiling anymore. I guess I'd have to say she looked comfortable, or something like that.

# Two Feet in One Shoe

Mary Sasarro hurried over the narrow dirt path, past the old abandoned house, a fine spray of dust following close on her heels like a swarm of bees. With each step her large bosom rose and fell against her body. Anybody could see Mary was upset. Her face was flushed and glistened in the morning light. "Strike me dead, your ass!" she said aloud. There wasn't anyone to hear her, except the old house sitting back off the path, looking pale and gaunt, with morning shadows from the tall oak trees creeping across skeleton windows, the glass long hollowed out by vandals.

Mary stopped in front of the once-landscaped walkway leading up to the house. In past years, Mary never gave the house a second look. The only time she used the path, a shortcut between Elizabeth and Catherine Streets, was on her way to visit her sister who lived on the other side of the property everyone called "the old house." But this morning, she noticed the front door, a massive paneled oak, leaning ajar like an unsteady old man. Only a rusting hinge kept the door from falling. Rays of sunlight drifted through the windows lighting patches of bare walls inside the rooms.

And all around the house, a garden withered, with struggling fruit trees, an old stone well, and quiet.

"Strike me dead, your ass!" she said aloud again, breaking the silence as though she knew the house would understand her anger and not fault her for remembering the night before.

Mary had been on her hands and knees scrubbing her kitchen floor, when the kitchen door opened and her husband stood in the doorway. He just stood there, lean and bent, stripes of sweat sucking the top of his BVD's to his body. He clutched a straw hat in his hand.

"Joe, whadda ya doing home so early from work? You don't feel good?"

Joe started to walk into the room.

"Wait a minute," Mary yelled, "wait till I get some paper down. You're gonna track dirt all over my clean floor." But Joe paid no attention to the wet floor and walked over to the kitchen table. "I lost my job." he said.

"What do you mean," she squinted, "you lost your job?"

"I mean just what I said. I lost my job. Understand? Carney says to me, 'We don't need you no more, Joe.'"

Mary looked at him, "Whadda we gonna do if we have no money coming in?" she asked.

"I'll get another job," he said.

"With who?" she mocked. "Who's gonna hire you? You're an old man. A washerwoman. All day your mouth goes. Like a fish."

"Please," he said. "Shut up, Mary. I got enough troubles."

Mary slowly rose and sat on one of the chairs lining the wall where she had put them until she was finished washing the floor. Joe put his lunch pail and hat on the table, and then he went to the sink and rinsed his face with cold water.

"What about the house? Are we gonna lose the house?" Mary folded her arms across her chest.

"We ain't gonna lose the house," Joe said splashing water on his body.

"How are we gonna pay the taxes?" she asked.

Joe rubbed himself down with the towel. "We'll pay the taxes."

But Mary was not convinced. "Why did God do this to us? You know why, because there is no God, no God."

Joe quickly blessed himself, elaborately making the sign of the cross with a dirt-darkened hand. "Don't talk like that, Mary. Do you want God to strike you dead?"

Mary's face turned red. He wasn't listening. She was losing

her house, the only thing she had ever owned in her life. And he wasn't listening. He heard only her sacrilege.

"Strike me dead, your ass," she screamed at him.

Now up ahead through a scrim of tall honeysuckle bushes, her sister's house—a yellow stucco structure—sparkled in the early morning sun. Such a fine house, she thought. Such a fine spot for a house, clean and quiet. Her own little bungalow over on the corner of Jane and Catherine Streets was wedged between Uncle Jack—who lived with a mulatto mistress and a yard full of scrap iron, goats and a donkey—and the large Catania family with twelve kids who lived in the rambling wooden house surrounded by litter, old cars, and junk of every description. Every day, Mary pulled the shades, so she did not have to look at the mess the kids left. Why couldn't they be like the Rosas up the road, they took care of their yard. It looked like her Joe's, nice and neat, you could sit there all day.

When Mary got to her sister's house, she stood outside the kitchen door and listened for any sound from within to let her know someone was at home. It was quiet, so she turned the knob. It opened at her touch.

"Jenny," she called. She waited. Again. "Jenny, are you home?"

This time a voice from the kitchen answered, "Come up. I'm home, where would I be?"

Mary entered the small kitchen. A short, plump woman in a flowered house dress stood in the middle of the kitchen sink washing a venetian blind.

"Are you crazy, Jenny, you fall out of that sink and you'll kill yourself," Mary scolded.

Jenny ignored Mary's concern and continued to wipe down each of the slats with a wet rag.

"I said to my kids, if you're going to get me something for Christmas, get me some shades for the kitchen windows. Shades, I said, nice dark green shades, so they give me these damn blinds. Do you want a cup of coffee?" she asked. "Check the pot, see if there's any left."

"It's stale, and I don't want stale coffee," Mary said and took the coffee pot off the stove. "Now how am I going to wash this pot and get some water with you in that sink?"

"Give it to me, for God's sake, and I'll fill it," Jenny said. "When I saw you coming past the old house I said to myself, here comes trouble. Look at you. Your blood pressure must be up, and your sugar must be up. What's wrong?"

"Joe lost his job. I'm going to lose my house, Jenny. I want you to buy my house and let me live in it until I die, then you can sell it." By now, Mary had put a pot of coffee on and had sat down at the table and was watching her sister finish cleaning the blinds.

"Are you out of your mind or something? Buy your house in that dump."

Mary glared at her sister. "My house is no dump!"

"I didn't say your house was a dump. I said where you live is a dump. Between Uncle Jack and his junk and the Catania family and those twelve rotten kids, who wants to live there? Who wants to hear Mrs. Catania yelling at those kids all day and the old man running after them with a shovel. It's a crazy house. What you should do, dear sister, is sell it to Mrs. Catania. How many times did you say she wants the house for her Mikey?"

Mary busied herself with pouring coffee and getting milk from the icebox. "I want to live there, Jenny." Mary said quietly. "I never had a house I owned before. It's mine, Jenny. I own it like other people. I pay taxes just like you and everybody else. I'm somebody, too."

Mary had lost all her anger now, she was feeling the loss, the meaning of her life slipping away. "I just wanted you to buy it, so I could stay there at least, and nobody could put me out till I die. That's all I wanted, Jenny."

Jenny had stepped out of the sink and sat at the table. "Listen to me, my sister, give it up. Go live with your daughter, Katie. She and Sam will take good care of you and Joe. You won't have to worry about anything. Do it. Give it up."

"I can't go and live with Katie," Mary said.

"Whadda ya mean, you can't live with Katie; that's crazy talk."

Mary said, "She's married to a Jew."

"Since when is Sammy a Jew?" Jenny asked. "You love him."

"I do, I do, he's like a son to me, he's...sometimes he puts his arms around me and he winks—you know how he winks his eyes—and he says, 'Ma, you're just like a Jewish mother.'"

"Then what's the matter?"

"It's his sister."

"You're not going to live with his sister."

"Yeh, but she lives in the apartment right across the hall from Katie, and Katie says she's always coming over to make sure Katie is doing this and doing that, like is she using the plates right."

"So, when she comes over, you go to your room; then you don't have to listen."

"Oh, Jenny, please how you talk! It's so easy for you. Your Annie married an Italian. A nice Catholic, Italian. All you have to worry about is you don't eat meat on Friday. You don't eat meat on Friday, you don't go to hell. I go to live with Katie, then I'll have to listen to Sam's God tell me what plate to eat my meat on. If I make a mistake, what happens to me? I'm too old, Jenny, for this."

"Mary," Jenny said as though she were talking to a child, slowly, in a low voice, "go home, let it go, forget it, start over. You're always making a mountain where there's no dirt."

Mary drank her coffee and stared ahead. "Jenny," she said, very quietly, as though she would be overheard. "Jenny, how come nobody lives in the old house?"

"You're changing the subject. You don't want to hear the truth."

"I'm listening to what you're saying, Jenny, but I just want to know how come nobody lives in the old house."

"I can't believe you don't know the story. About the poor man who built the house for his wife in Germany, and she died before she could come over and live in it. It was sad, very sad. The poor man just left, went away and never came back."

Mary thought about what her sister said. "And nobody takes care of it. It's just falling down, and nobody cares."

"The man who lives up on the corner is supposed to take care of it, but . . . you know, it's not his house, so he don't care."

Mary sighed. "I wish, Jenny, somebody had loved me like that. Maybe Frank did love me like that, but I never had a chance to find out. You didn't know Frank DeMartini was my boyfriend once, before I married Joe. You didn't know that did you?" Mary bent over the table and looked right at Jenny, who was not comfortable with the conversation.

"That was a long time ago, Mary, a lot of things happened a long time ago. What's the good of bringing it all up now?"

"Because I wanted to tell you. After all, you're my sister. Who else can I tell? I want you to know something about me, something special. I can't tell Joe, my kids don't care, and I need to tell somebody now."

Jenny rose from the table and began to remove the cups. She said nothing. "We were in love, yes, we were, Jenny." Mary continued. I was just sixteen and he was nineteen and we used to talk about running away and getting married just as soon as Frank had enough money saved up. But Joe—remember how he used to come to the house to see Pa?—well, he told Pa he wanted me and Pa, he didn't care about us. Tells him, sure he could marry me, and that was it, Jenny. I had nothing to say about it. The next thing I was married, and Joe brought me here to the house. In those days, Pa could do that. You were lucky you married the man you wanted."

"All right, now you got it off your chest, go home, make peace with your troubles. We do what we haffta do, Mary. It's always been like that, since the day Ma died and we were babies and Pa married Stepmother, who never cared if we lived or died. You and me, Mary, we always had to walk with two feet in one shoe, but we make the best."

Later, when Mary left the house she took the narrow path again, past the old house.

This time she was in no hurry. She found a patch of grass facing the house and sat down. "It's a damn shame. That's all I have to say: it's a damn shame. Such a nice old house you used to be, but nobody cares if you fall down; they don't even remember what you looked like." Mary shook her head. "So whadda ya gonna do? When the time comes, that's it."

She picked herself up, dusted off her cotton dress and started for home.

Joe was weeding in the flower garden that was like a fence around the house. Mary said nothing to him. She went into the house and called Katie. Mary explained about the job, her fears and said, "When I sell the house, you can put a down payment on that nice little bungalow in Cliff Park, the one with the two bedrooms you looked at and wished you could afford. Well, you can, if me and your father can come and live with you. We won't be any trouble. We'll help you. Your father can make a nice garden and help around the yard, and I can cook when you go to work. It will be nice, you'll see. What do you think, Katie? Sammy, he'll like it; I know Sammy, he's a good man."

Katie was fine with the idea, jumped at it and said Sammy would be happy too. "Go ahead," she told her mother, "See if the old lady next door still wants to buy the house for her Mikey."

The next morning Mary woke early. She went to the closet and took out her only fancy dress, black with red roses across the hem and neckline. She took a pair of silk stockings from the bureau drawer.

The bathroom was cold, but she washed all over and put on the dress and stockings, rolling the stockings down till they looked like doughnuts around her ankles. She found her patent leather shoes, wiped away the dust and put them on. Without even looking in the small mirror that hung over the bathroom sink, she combed her hair and pulled it back from her face with a large tortoiseshell pin. Grabbing her purse, she was ready to leave the house.

Joe was reading the El Progresso paper and he looked up when she came into the kitchen.

"Where you going, all dressed up? It's not even Sunday."

"To talk with Mrs. Catania. I'll be back in a while."

"What for? Mary, what are you doing? Why are you going to talk to Mrs. Catania? You didn't say anything to me first."

Mary left as though he weren't even in the room.

It was just a short walk over to Mrs. Catania's house. Mary knocked on the door and waited. A short, very heavy woman came to the door, and when she saw Mary, she smiled broadly. "Mary, hey, what are you doing out so early. Come in, come in."

Mary entered a large kitchen that smelled of spaghetti sauce and garlic. But the room was sunny, and clean and coffee perked on the stove.

"I want to talk to you about my house," Mary said.

Mrs. Catania had been friendly and happy to see Mary, but now she took Mary by the arm and showed her a chair.

"Sit, Mary, sit."

Mrs. Catania had put a white mug on the table, but when Mary mentioned the word *house*, she removed the mug and went to the kitchen cupboard and took out two small china cups and saucers with matching sugar bowl and creamer. Before putting them on the table, she spread a white linen tablecloth over it.

Mary sat still and watched Mrs. Catania bring the coffee pot to the table.

"Now, Mary, fresh coffee. Let's drink."

Mary took a sip.

"Good, Mrs. Catania, very good."

# Rachel #5

Mama never should have rented out my side of the double bed. The one I shared with my older sister Annie. Even if the new boarder was a fortune teller who paid Mama ten dollars a week.

I tried to talk to Annie about it. She's sixteen, four years older than me, and all she thinks about is her Johnny. He's her steady boyfriend.

"Mama can do whatever she wants. No skin off my nose," Annie said.

"Yeh, Annie, but now I'm gonna have to sleep with Joey, and he kicks all night. I'll be black and blue for the rest of my life."

Joey was our four-year-old brother, and sometimes he even wet the bed.

"Soooo," Annie said. "What about me? You think I'm gonna have a swell time? I'll have to sleep with a perfect stranger. What if she hogs the bed, or puts her cold feet on me?"

Well, anyway, it didn't seem to matter a bit what either one of us thought, 'cause there was Frieda Miller that cold January afternoon, all round and pink, sitting in our parlor drinking coffee with Mama. She was wearing something filmy the color of lilacs and violets and purple, like the color of the vestments Father Mahoney wears to say Mass during Lent. Two of her men friends were with her. They were dressed in black suits, and all I could think of when I saw them was that movie, The Mark of the Vampire.  She never brought them around again, and, boy, was I glad because I didn't want to have to look at them and think of vampires.

Annie said they probably spent the afternoon having seances. Mama liked all that kind of stuff, you know. Everybody in the whole world knew Mama carried a horseshoe in her purse when she went to play Bingo, and a rabbit's foot on a string around her neck for good luck.

"A bunch of junk," Annie says. "Nobody is coming back from the grave to talk to Mama. Anyway, who cares?"

Annie is such a know-it-all, thinks she knows everything. Even Mama thinks so. She treats Annie like she was the mother and Mama was the kid.

"Well, you don't know everything, Annie," I let her know.

She can really be a pain, she turns everything I think upside down and gets me in trouble. She laughs at me when I read fairy tales and is always snitching to Mama about my going to the library after school instead of coming straight home.

All this spirit stuff with a fortune teller sounded interesting to me.

So did Frieda.

The very first thing I noticed that afternoon was her mouth puckered into a bow, and her cheeks puffed out like she was blowing bubbles.

But best of all I liked her dress. Flowered chiffon, which went very well with her silk stockings and black high heels.

Her hair fell around her face in big, fat finger waves, the kind you get when you go to the beauty parlor. When we shook hands, I noticed Frieda's were soft, and her nails were pink and manicured, not like my mother's. Hers always looked like she was digging for potatoes.

Frieda smiled when I said hello, and she took my hand in hers.

"What's your name, dear?"

"Maria," I said.

"Maria. Oh, I like that name. It fits you, too." She kept patting my hand like I was a pet cat or something.

"We're going to be great friends."

I never had a fortune teller for a friend before. Actually, the only other fortune teller I knew was Mary Jack, the mulatto lady from New Orleans who lived with Uncle Jack over on Ann street in the bungalow next to Auntie Mary, who is Mama's only sister, real sister that is, 'cause Mama has a bunch of stepsisters and brothers, too. Well, Mama and Auntie Mary said we weren't allowed to talk to Mary Jack or look at her, like our eyes meeting or something. They said Mary Jack had evil powers and that she put Uncle Jack under a spell or he wouldn't be living in sin with a woman who wasn't his wife. Sound like one of those Grimm fairy tales I like so much.

Well then, Aunt Christina should have stayed home and not run off to Minnesota with her daughter, just because Uncle Jack likes clocks and keeps them all over the house, even on the kitchen sink.

Anyway, Frieda didn't look like she would cast spells on anybody, or anything like that, and right after school the next day, I hurried home.

Mama was in the kitchen making soup. I threw my bookbag on the table.

"Is Frieda still here?" I asked.

But Mama wasn't listening.

"Don't leave your bookbag on the table," she said. "Put it where it belongs." Mama never answers my questions.

So, I ran up the stairs to Frieda's room. The door was closed.

"Frieda, it's me, are you in there?"

"Come in, Maria."

Frieda was standing in front of the bureau looking at herself in the mirror. You know, turning her head this way and that, and the whole room smelled like the perfume counter at Mr. Levy's drugstore. Well, anyway sometimes the store smelled like perfume, but most of the time, the drugstore smelled like rubber enema bags.

On the bureau top in front of Frieda was a black leather case. The lid was up, and there were jars of lotions and rouges and bottles with labels that read "powder base" and "moisture cream."

On one round box, the same shade as the poppy flowers that grow in Mama's front yard, were the words Rachel #5 printed on top.

"What's in there?" I asked.

"That's my favorite face powder," Frieda said, and when she opened the box a whiff of powder escaped and settled on the bureau top. She held the box out so I could look into it. The powder looked so soft; I wanted to run my fingers through it like I do sometimes with the flour when Mama is making bread. Frieda dipped a soft, pink powder puff into the box and gently dabbed the powder on her nose, her cheeks, and her chin.

"See," she said, turning to me. "See how smooth it makes my skin? And the color, and the scent?" She took in a deep breath.

"It's so special," she said, "So special."

I think for a minute, she forgot I was there. She looked like she went far away.

I didn't get to see too much more of Frieda that first week. But by the weekend, Mama had bought a big bag of loose tea and, first thing Saturday morning, we had our first tea leaf reading. Frieda told Mama there was money in her cup, and Mama didn't say a word. But when you get to know her like I do, you can tell just by how Mama shapes her mouth, if she's glad or mad, and that Saturday morning, Mama sure was glad.

After that, every Saturday morning we drank tea for breakfast. Except my Papa of course—he said drinking tea was like drinking dishwater, so he still drank coffee, and Frieda put some coffee grounds in his cup so she could tell his fortune, too.

He didn't believe anything she said, not about little birds carrying messages in their beaks, or bunches of money coming into the house, or anything. He laughed when she told him he was going to get a raise. Papa never expects to get a raise, he said. He's happy, just to work for the Aluminum Company down by the river and glad to have a job. Then he'd go on about how the workers were trying hard to get a Union together, then maybe he would get a raise, but he seemed to like talking and laughing with Frieda, anyway.

One morning, I peered into my teacup trying to make out the shape of something down in there. Frieda said it was a bird, but all I saw was a mess of tea leaves. By spring, though, after all those Saturday readings, I told Frieda I saw the little bird, and I thought I saw other things following me up the stairs when I went to bed at night, too.

When I told her, her eyes lit up.

"Now, think carefully, darling. Are you sure it wasn't your shadow?"

"Oh, no, Frieda," I said. "It was small, and it had wings."

"Was it . . . like a dove?" Frieda's voice got very low.

"Yes," I said, almost in a whisper. I just knew that's what she wanted me to say, and so I did. Besides maybe I did see a dove.

"Oh, my dear, my dear," she cried. "You have it. You have been chosen."

Doves had something to do with purity, she said. I didn't know what she was talking about, but it was fun to think I was special.

Well, after that, we took lots of walks together, and I could talk to her about anything, you know, just like when you have a special friend from school. I told her about my boyfriends, who I liked and who I didn't. Like Walter from up the road, who lived with his uncle and aunt and had two very large front teeth. He liked to play hide-and-seek with us, but he always got left out and nobody wanted to hide with him, 'cause he always tried to kiss you, and nobody wanted to kiss him back. We were afraid he would bite us.

Frieda didn't laugh or make fun of me. She treated me just like I was grownup. Not like my sister, Annie. If I told her about Johnny Maggio who always smelled like garlic, she would have said, "Oh, please, don't bother me with that childish nonsense. So if you don't want to play with Johnny, tell him to go home and brush his teeth."

Well, things were going along pretty good at our house. The extra money Frieda contributed as a boarder helped a lot, what with the Depression and all.

Still Frieda and Mama never really got to be friends. Mama could have sat with Papa and Frieda out on the front stoop after supper, if she wanted to. But Mama wasn't one for talking and doing nothing. She thought it was a waste of time. Mama didn't have a frivolous bone in her body.

Before I knew it, school was out, and I could spend lots more time with Frieda, except when she was taking a nap. As the days grew hotter, Frieda wouldn't go for a walk, or shop, or do anything that took her outdoors in the middle of the day.

Even on Sundays, Frieda rested after dinner. Later in the afternoon, she would bathe, change her clothes, and put on fresh makeup, which I was never allowed to watch. Then she would ask Mama if she cared to go for a walk up to the cemetery or to the soda store. But Mama was always busy.

When Frieda asked Papa, he would put his arm around her. "Sure, it's a nice day for a walk." And they would go off together, laughing.

Mama just watched them through the window and muttered, "Well, I wish I had nothing else to do but go for a walk."

Sometimes I wished Mama would go, just to have some fun. She and Papa never seemed to have any fun together, but I guess that's the way it was.

One afternoon I was playing over at Auntie Mary's house with my cousins Katie and Rose. Auntie Mary was working in Cliffside that day cleaning house for those crazy ballet dancers. That's what Auntie Mary calls them, anyway, because they live in this big house full of canaries and parrots that fly all over the place and Auntie Mary has to clean up after them, and the ballet dancers never cook, Auntie said, they bring home supper from the delicatessen.

Well, me and my cousins went across the street to tease the goats grazing up on the hillside. It was getting late, and the sun seemed to just hang in the sky. Katie said she had to go home to start the beans for supper when I noticed the sunlight bouncing around on the kitchen window.

"Katie," I said, pointing. "What's that on your window?"

"I don't know," she said.

"Look. It's floating around like it's trying to get in. It could be a ghost," I said. It was probably a reflection off some old can in the garden, but I wanted it to be something scary.

"Now you scared me like anything, and I'm not going in that house before Mama comes home," Katie said. Rose was almost in tears.

"Maybe we should ask Mary Jack what it is?" I said. We looked at each other, like "Let's do it," and we ran down the hill to Mary Jack's house. She was sitting on her front porch in a rocking chair, dressed in a long white skirt with a red flowered shirt, and her feet were bare and long. Her white hair was pulled back straight off her face and her eyes were closed. She never even bothered to open them when she asked us what we wanted.

"What you kids standing there at the gate for, looking at Mary Jack? Didn't your Mamas tell you never to speak to Mary Jack?"

I poked Katie and whispered in her ear, "G'wan, ask her anyway."

"All right," Katie said. "We're sorry to bother you, Mary Jack, but there's a ball of light floating around on my kitchen window, and Mama's not home. and we're scared to go in the house,'cause maybe it's a ghost or something and we thought maybe you would come with us?"

Mary Jack just let out a big laugh.

"Come over to your house? Sooner walk into a snake pit," she said. Her eyes were still closed, and she kept right on rocking.

"You tell your Ma that spirit wanted to give her a message." Mary Jack opened her eyes and leaned forward in the chair and there was this smile on her face. "It was your grandpa." She said, talking kind of slow. "He's sorry. Yeh, he sorry for all the bad things he done to her, for stepmother, and everything." Then she leaned back in her chair again, closed her eyes and she had a big smile on her face.

"Grandpa would never come to Auntie Mary's house." I poked Katie.

"She said if he ever did, she would throw him down the well."

I just said what came to my mind. I forgot all about being afraid of Mary Jack. But I just knew it couldn't have been Grandpa. Auntie Mary said she would never forgive him for being such a rotten father. And he never came when he was alive, so I couldn't understand why he would come now that he was dead.

"Katie, come on, let's go." I pulled her away from the gate, "Your mom's gonna be home any minute and we're gonna be in trouble."

"You kids, go on. Get out of here and leave Mary Jack alone, and don't come back again," she called after us. As we ran away, we could hear Mary Jack laughing and singing one of those songs she sings when she works in the garden and she raises her voice so loud you can hear her clear up to the cemetery, singing about rivers and Jesus and stuff like that. But she couldn't have been too mad at us. She didn't do anything bad. Anyway, maybe Mama was wrong about her turning kids into frogs. Maybe she doesn't even think of doing things like that.

The next morning, I was in the pantry cleaning out the icebox when I heard Auntie Mary's voice talking to Mama. Sounded like they were coming into the kitchen.

"I am telling you, Jenny, the kids went over to Mary Jack."

"After all we told them about her . . . ." Mama didn't sound happy.

"Katie said it was because your Maria said she saw something trying to get in my kitchen window. It's all this ghosts and spirits and fortune telling stuff going on around here."

"So, what are you saying?" I heard Mama ask Auntie Mary, and she sounded a little strange.

"Get rid of that woman, that Frieda, or you're going to be sorry. She's filling up that kid's head with a lot of nonsense and . . . ." Auntie Mary's voice stopped.

"And, what?" Mama asked.

"I wasn't going to say this, but . . . she's after your husband."

I waited to hear what Mama would say, but she didn't say anything, and then she changed the subject.

I asked my sister about it later that day. "Annie, does that mean Mama and Papa are going to get a divorce?"

"How do I know? Anyway, what does Auntie Mary know about it? Maybe Frieda and Papa are just friends. Why do you always ask me such dumb questions?"

I was a little scared. I didn't want to live with just one parent, like the Flaherty kids. They live with their father, and they only see their mother when she comes on the trolley car and gets off on Main Street.

Well anyway, the following Saturday, Mama announced there

would be no more readings. Frieda was disappointed, but I didn't say anything. Mama's mouth looked mad.

But Frieda and Papa still laughed a lot and took walks together in the evening. Frieda and I were still friends. I just couldn't stop talking to her, but I noticed that she and Papa spent more time together, and I didn't see her as much as I used to. I even felt sorry for Mama. She didn't seem to be having any fun, and all she had was the extra money every week.

The summer was dry and hot. Mama didn't stop doing things around the house, just like always. And Frieda still took her afternoon naps. On Sunday mornings, she went to church with us, always looking fresh and polished in a starched cotton or a breezy print dress and open-toed sandals. Mama hardly ever talked to her at all now.

Then in the month of August, Papa brought home tickets to the Democratic Party's annual bus ride to Asbury Park. There was one for Frieda, too.

The day of the excursion the weather was just right. The sun was shining, and it was hot: just right for a trip to the beach. I was excited. I always liked the bus rides, going to a new place, meeting boys. Frieda looked real cool in a yellow sundress, and she had on a wide straw hat. Mama looked like she always did, as though she were going to clean the house or something.

Katie and Rose came, too, and we spent the day splashing in and out of the ocean, eating hot dogs, and looking for boys. Toward the end of the day, Mama asked me to look for Papa.

"Tell him I need help getting all this stuff to the bus. We'll be leaving soon."

I ran down the beach checking out people lying on the sand and under the boardwalk. I just kept running until I got to where there were hardly any more people on the beach. When I looked under the boardwalk ahead of me, I saw Frieda and Papa. They were sitting on a rock real close to each other just like people do in the movies.

I didn't feel so good.

"Papa," I yelled. They turned and saw me.

"Mama wants you!" I yelled.

He backed away from Frieda, and when he stopped in front of me, I couldn't tell whether he was mad or scared. And then he said in a voice like I better listen carefully, "It was nothing, you hear? Nothing."

Then he headed down the beach. I just stood there.

Frieda called, "Maria."

She started walking out from underneath the boardwalk.

"I don't want to talk to you," I said, backing up. "What were you and Papa doing?"

"Nothing, Maria. Just talking about the ocean and what a beautiful day it is, things like that."

"I don't believe you. Auntie Mary is right. You're after my father."

"Oh, no, no, no. This isn't what you think. Please, believe me. Your father, we're . . . we're just friends. And we were just playing, just playing, that's all."

"You're lying, just like those lies you see in the teacup. And you're ugly" I said, and I looked for more words to hurt her, "And all that rouge and Rachel powder you put on your face doesn't make you pretty. You're old and ugly, and you're not my friend, and I don't ever want to see you again."

I kept walking backwards until I could feel my feet being sucked into the wet sand near the water's edge.

"And all that junk about being special . . . You lied to me. You lie about everything. I hate you."

"No, no, Maria. You are special.

"You're bad. My mother didn't do anything to you. You leave my father alone."

I turned and ran down the wet beach, trying to keep back the tears. I didn't want my mother asking me questions, so I stopped and splashed water on my face.

If Mama ever suspected what happened, she didn't say anything except to tell everyone what they should carry back to the bus. On the way home, I sat in a seat with my brother. Papa sat with Mama and was very quiet and didn't look at me at all.

Frieda sat up front and talked to the bus driver. I even heard her laugh once in a while.

The next morning, I got up early and told Mama I was going to spend the day at Auntie Mary's with Katie and Rose. I didn't want to be there with Frieda. I didn't want to talk to her or see her or anything. Katie and Rose kept asking me why I was such a sourpuss all day, but I couldn't tell them about Papa and Frieda.

Later, when I came home, Mama was in the backyard weeding the vegetable garden with my brother Joey. So I went into the house. It was quiet. But like a different quiet. It was like the day we all came home from Uncle Louie's funeral and, when we walked into his house, everything was so still, like it was stiff, like the house was frozen. Like it died too.

I went upstairs, real slow. I didn't know what was up there. Frieda and Annie's bedroom door was open halfway, and I could see the foot of the bed. The mattress had been stripped. I walked in and looked around. Her side of the closet was empty. The late afternoon sun splashed across the bureau top, and a thin layer of powder made an outline where the makeup box had been.

I stood there and looked at the powder. Slowly I ran my fingers through the dust. I closed my eyes and touched my face. I drew in a deep breath. Such a sweet perfume. So special. I was going to miss Rachel #5. I was going to miss it a lot.

# Putting On the Dog

Mama just loved to put on the dog. You know, act like she was raised with white damask tablecloths draped over polished mahogany tables and ladies dressed in silk and cultured pearls serving mashed potatoes from china bowls.

Guess it might have had something to do with Mama being born on Nanny Goat Hill, not wearing shoes all summer, and never learning to read or write.

She left home one day when she was sixteen and went to live with her married sister. Just walked out and never so much as gave it another thought. Left it all behind her. Stepmother. Grandpa. The gray stone house with dark rooms. The noisy streets. Being hungry. Going out to work when she was just thirteen, when all she wanted to do was go to school. Having nothing. Just bare feet and goats.

Well, she couldn't help hearing people talk about those movie stars and about people making movies in the small town not too far from Nanny Goat Hill. Everybody knew about it. Big business, they said. Well, that's when she decided she'd leave, just move out as though anybody would have cared anyway, and get a job in one of those movie places. Well, one day she said she was going to check on the goats grazing over on the hill, and she just walked away, kept right on walking 'til she got to her sister's house, where she stayed 'til she met my father.

Still, Nanny Goat Hill had a hold on Mama kind of like it had her caught by the belt on her cotton dress. Never stopped tugging at her.

Sometimes Mama went back to the Hill to a funeral or something like that, but hardly anyone from Nanny Goat Hill ever came to our house except Uncle Carnie and his new bride the night they eloped and spent the first night with us, and we had to do some fancy moving around finding enough beds for all of us to sleep in so Uncle Carnie and Rosemary could be alone.

When Mama was with anybody from Nanny Goat Hill, she sounded just like them: you know, loud and her voice was sort of sing-songy. You'd never know she was the same person who thought it was high class to turn a perfectly "Good morning" into "Good merning," and say "of curse" instead of "of course."

But no matter how many times we told her, "It's 'morning,' Mama. Say M-O-R-E, more-ning. And please don't purse your lips and spit out your words like they were pinched together." We might just as well have talked to our old hunting dog, Brownie. He's deaf.

She'd still turn around and say, "Good merning." To her it sounded high class.

You know, lots of people—like those ladies from the Women's Republican Club and the Holy Rosary Sodality—well, after a while I guess they didn't notice Mama putting on the dog. They just thought Mama was pretty incredible, not knowing how to read and all, getting out there and doing just fine with the hoity-toities and acting as though she was Mrs. Fort Hill, New Jersey.

So, on weekdays at home, Mama wore a flowered cotton house dress, and on Republican meeting days, she put on a corset and the black rayon dress she bought on sale at Macy's one day when she got off the subway at the wrong stop. She was going to 14th street but got off a little too soon and, instead of going to Norton's, she wound up at Macy's on a sale day.

Well, anyway, one day the Depression was going on and we were all having a hard time, but we really didn't have time to think about it, 'cause it wasn't all "going on relief," you know, buying groceries with a piece of paper the town gave you that entitled you to some free food, but it wasn't exactly a charlotte russe with inches of whipped cream down at Setzer's Bakery, either.

But if anybody was going to survive the Depression, it would be Mama. 'Cause, I tell you, she was like Jesus Christ and the miracle of the loaves and fishes. She had a bureau drawer she somehow filled with dimes and nickels and at the beginning of every month, when Mr. O'Malley came to collect for the Metropolitan Insurance Co., and Mr. Tamburelli collected for the Prudential Insurance Co., and Johnny Mullins came collecting for John Hancock, it was like a miracle. All the nickels and dimes she needed were there. She even had enough to pay Mr. Shear, the old Jewish peddler who came during the summer months and sold Mama and the neighborhood women everything they needed for their daughters' hope chests: sheets, towels, nightgowns, tablecloths. And for the ladies—with lots of giggles—wide-legged, pink, rayon bloomers.

Well, anyway, my sister Annie—that's my older sister, she's seventeen—she brought home this new boyfriend, Michael. Oh, my, he had a very big nose. I mean this nose just went on and on. Well not that big, but from the side as he sat in his tan Ford sedan, he was all nose. He had a nice head of hair, too, thick and wavy, but until you got to know him, he was Mr. Nose.

Annie really liked Michael. In the beginning, Michael was shy, like a little dog—didn't want to get out of the car and come in to meet Annie's family. But once he did, well, we just forgot all about his nose and thought Annie had got herself a real catch. I mean, she didn't have to be ashamed to show him off. Not like that other guy she was going with, Nicky. He was cute, oh, yeh, but he had this smell, like the salamis that hung from the ceiling in his father's grocery store. Of course, Mama, knew Michael's father before Mama married our father. His name was Charlie, Michael's father, and he had been Mama's boss at the film factory. What a feather in Mama's cap—her old boss's son about to be her son-in-law.

"So," Mama said to Annie. "Going out with Charlie Maroni's son, huh? You act nice, now." Mama was afraid Annie would do something stupid, like the time she and the entire freshman

Home Economics class did a tap dance on the school stage in red-and-blue checkered shorts and a halter. A halter! With their backs out. Bare backs! Annie said they were just trying to show the school and the parents what they could do, how well they could sew in Home Economics. But some people in town—and Annie said she coulda cared less about them—said she was practically a prostitute. Well, not to Mama's face, of course, and after a while everybody forgot about it. Still Mama wanted Annie to know she was to watch her p's and q's if she was going out with Michael Maroni.

Mama liked Mr. Maroni. "He's nice," she said. "But his wife, phew. Her nose is up in the air. Charlie's too good for her."

"I'm not marrying Mrs. Maroni," Annie said. "Anyway Mr. Maroni likes me, so anything she says can't hurt me." Annie knew just where to plant her feet on solid ground. Always did. Had a lot of Mama in her.

Pretty soon, Annie and Michael were looking and talking like they were getting ready to be married. Mama had started a hope chest when Annie was only fourteen, 'cause she just knew Annie would marry young. The cedar chest in Mama's bedroom was bulging like an overstuffed cow with bedspreads and draperies and nightgowns and slips and towels and, oh, my, all the fifty cents and dollars that Mama put into that stuff.

So, one day, Annie told Mama she wanted to have Mr. and Mrs. Maroni over for afternoon coffee; it was time for the two families to get together. You could see that Mama was excited. I mean having Mr. and Mrs. Maroni over for coffee, well, Mama had come a long way from just being a worker in the film factory. She was going to be Michael Maroni's mother-in-law. Family. Well, you might say.

Mama didn't plan on putting on the dog with Mrs. Maroni. She never does. It comes sort of natural, like putting your shoe on the right foot. All week, Mama and Annie cleaned and shined things up with lemon oil, scrubbed and waxed floors, put lace curtains on the stretcher to dry, and Mama got out the Made-in-Japan Satsuma cups and saucers with the cake plates to match. She even took out the artificial flowers wrapped and stored in the china cabinet for special occasions and put them in a vase on the dining room table.

The house looked pretty good, just like it does for Christmas when we spend all the weekends in December cleaning and scrubbing and washing windows till our hands are ready to fall off from the cold.

So, the day of the coffee with the Maronis came. A beautiful late fall day. The sun sparkled through those clean windows, and with everything rubbed down with lemon oil, the house just shone like magic. Mama put on her corset, her black dress, and silk stockings. You just had to see her: she looked beautiful. You know Mama is really a nice looking woman when she's all dressed up. I remember she came to a PTA meeting one Sunday when my class had to put on a program for the parents. She had on her black dress and a pearl necklace and she wore a black straw hat that had large white flowers pinned to it. I was so proud of her that day, and I prayed real quiet to myself, please Mary, Mother of God, just don't let her get up and speak,'causeif she just sat there, nice and quiet, you'd never guess she didn't grow up with damask tablecloths.

Well, the day the Maronis came over, Mama didn't waste any time. She put on a pot of coffee to perk and sliced a loaf of Tayste pound cake, the one with raisins, and put it on a matching Satsuma dish. Oh, the excitement was really high. Papa, who all these months stayed out of all this, put on a white shirt and scrubbed his hands to get some of the dirt out from under his nails.

Papa didn't like just hanging around. Doing nothing made him nervous, and when he got nervous he'd have a drink of wine or a shot of homemade whiskey that he kept in the wine cellar in the basement, and sometimes he got a little too friendly. With the women, that is. And a friendly pinch here and there made Mama cross.

So, she reminded him. "You watch how you act today when the Maronis come, and don't you do nothing stupid to Mrs. Maroni. You know, they ain't like us. They hang around with big shots who know how to act." But Papa assured her he had no intention of pinching Mrs. Maroni's ass. "So don't worry about it."

At exactly two o'clock, Michael and his parents were at the door. Annie let them in and Charlie Maroni called out to Mama, "Jenny, good to see you. Been a long time." Mama smiled a tight little smile, one of her high-class smiles.

"Jenny, this is my wife, Angela. Angela, this is Jenny. She used to work for me at the Paragon, and a damn good worker she was, too."

Well, you had to see this with your own eyes. Mama had extended her hand to Mrs. Maroni and was smiling one of those squeezed smiles, saying, "Pleased to meetcha." But Angela Maroni just stood there with her hands folded in front of her and all she said was, "Jenny."

Mama didn't say a word. She dropped her hand pretty fast and just pursed her lips and said, "Sit down, wontcha."

But you could see Mama had no use for Angela. And Angela, well, she had to be here, that's all there was to it, so . . .

Papa, on the other hand, smiled and shook hands and was quite friendly. Then they all sat down. Charlie leaned back on the couch and crossed his legs. Papa leaned forward and rested his elbows on his legs. Angela sat up as straight as a ruler in the Morris chair and crossed her feet. And Mama, she sat on the edge of the Mission oak side chair and looked like she was ready to take off after one of the chickens running around in the chicken coop.

The conversation was just about what you'd expect. How was the weather? They could use some rain. Wasn't the time going fast, before you know it, Thanksgiving would be there? They just, you know, talked at each other, 'cause what was Mama and Papa going to talk about to the Maronis, who lived on the Palisades in a big Victorian house, owned two cars, hobnobbed with movie people, and ate at the New York Athletic Club? I mean, what could they talk about? Michael and Annie sat on the couch close to each other, holding hands and stealing little kisses, and didn't seem to remember that anyone else was around.

Pretty soon, they all ran out of things to say, and Mama jumped up and said she'd get the coffee. Angela, who hadn't said a word the whole time, just sat there like the stick that holds up the green beans in Mama's garden and gave one of those smiles that had no heart in it.

After a while, when they were drinking their coffee, Papa and Mr. Maroni got on fine talking about Franklin Roosevelt. Course Papa just loved Franklin Roosevelt, but Mr. Maroni was knocking the WPA— that's what everybody called the Work Progress Administration for short—and Papa was getting right back at him, 'cause if it wasn't for the WPA, Papa said we'd have starved to death.

Then like a siren waking you up in the middle of the night, we heard the telephone ring, and Mama jumped up and ran to the kitchen to answer it. Then we could hear Mama's voice, loud. "The Feds! Jesus, Mary, and Joseph. All right. Yeh. Thank you. We'll tell 'em and get rid of it."

Mama came tearing into the living room. Her face was red, and she had forgotten all about the Maronis and being high class. She headed straight for my father.

"Tony, that was Chief Malloy. He says to get rid of the whiskey, the Feds are on their way out from Hackensack. It had to be that rotten Hun across the street that snitched. Who else would do it?"

"Brutta bestia!" Papa yelled. "Lutherans! If they drank a little grappa now and then and didn't have so many bake sales, maybe they'd be better off."

He looked at Mr. Maroni. "You want to help? We got a lot of bottles to move."

Sure. Mr. Maroni didn't have any love for Lutherans either. It seemed to bother Mr. Maroni that the Lutherans in his town had a minister who was an insurance man.

"Would you go to Confession, tell your sins to an insurance man?"

Papa laughed, and Mr. Maroni followed him down the cellar steps while Mama called out the back window to Sabina, who lived right next door, to get rid of the whiskey, the Feds were coming, and would she please call over to Bruno and tell him, too, just in case the Feds decided to check out all three houses.

Then Mama cautiously asked Mrs. Angela Maroni, who was still sitting on the chair with her back up straight as a rod, "Would you like to come down and help, Mrs. Maroni?"

At the same time, Mama took notice of the shoes Mrs. Maroni was wearing—high heels. Spiked high heels. Well, she couldn't go too far out in the backyard, carrying jugs of whiskey across the stream and into the woods. "You could get the bottles down from the shelf in the wine cellar and hand them to the men."

Mrs. Maroni at first shook her head, no, she would wait where she was. Mama was disappointed but just said, maybe a little sarcastic, "That's okay. You don't wanna to help, you don't hafta help."

Then Mrs. Maroni stood up. "No, you don't understand. I would like to, but...." She never finished the sentence. There was a look on her face, like she wanted to tell Mama something, but instead she put her purse down on the chair and said, "Please, just show me what I can do."

Mama led Mrs. Maroni down the steps to the wine cellar and showed her where the bottles of whiskey were and what to do. The men had already started taking bottles and hiding them in the woods across the stream in back of the house. As they came back from the woods, Mrs. Maroni handed them bottles of whiskey, anisette, liquors, and they did the leg-work down the garden path, across the stream, and into the trees. They just carried bottle after bottle across that stream until all the bottles were safely hidden away. Papa still had the copper still in the cellar, so he and Mr. Maroni carried that out, too. Then they left to help Sabina and Bruno.

Mama had been running back and forth with the men, and when they left, she went back to the wine cellar to thank Mrs. Maroni. Angela was sitting on one of the shelves that held the wine barrels, and she looked like a little kid waiting to get scolded for wetting her pants. She had her hands folded in her lap. Her body looked as tight as a spring. Something had happened, something Mama never would have expected. But as soon as Mrs. Maroni started talking, Mama knew Mrs. Maroni had been tasting the whiskey.

"But the liquors looked so interesting. . ." Angela wiped at her face, muttering. "The way they were bottled, with all those little cherries and things in there."

You could see there was a lot of activity going on in Mama's head, but she didn't have a chance to say anything stupid, 'cause Mrs. Maroni blurted out, "He's going to give me hell."

Well, Mama was right on top of that. "Look," she said, " I don't know what goes on between you and Charlie and I don't want to, but I don't see any reason he'd give you hell. Tasting a little bit of whiskey ain't no mortal sin."

"You don't understand," Mrs. Maroni said, averting Mama's in-your-face look.

Then just as serious as a funeral obituary, Mrs. Maroni lifted up her head, looked Mama straight in the eye, and said, "It's not what you think at all. You see, I'm allergic to alcohol. It affects my equilibrium, and Charles, poor dear, worries about me."

Well, Mama didn't know too much about a word like equilibrium, but she knew what Mrs. Maroni's problem was. Even if one day Mama was putting on the dog and another day cursing out Monsignor Murphy for sending her an annual Offering Envelope to support the church, Mama knew who Mama was. And if Mrs. Angela Maroni had to please those people at the Country Club and the fancy houses on the Palisades, well that wasn't very important 'cause it didn't put any food on Mama's table. Mama's favorite advice, when I worried what prissy Muriel thought of a hat I had to wear to church or how I look with my hair cut up to my ears, was, "Those people ain't no better than you. Do you owe them money? Well, if you don't, then you don't have to worry what they think."

So, Mama took Mrs. Maroni's arm and led her up the stairs and over to the armchair.

"Sit down," she said. "I'll make us a nice fresh pot of coffee. Don't that sound nice?" She didn't wait around to hear what Mrs. Maroni had to say, and a little later Mama brought back a mug of hot coffee and put it in Mrs. Maroni's hand.

"Here, try this. You'll just smell like coffee. And put up your feet, make yourself comfortable." Mama brought over the footstool and put Mrs. Maroni's feet on it.

"I am not feeling too good, and Charlie is going to know I drank some of that stuff as soon as I open my mouth. He'll smell it on my breath."

Mrs. Maroni didn't sound so good, either. "I have a headache."

"Good," Mama said. "Just tell Mr. Maroni you're not feeling good and you have a headache and don't talk too much."

"Oh, he'll notice," Mrs. Maroni said. "He may not say anything here, but wait till I get home."

You could tell Mama didn't like to see Mrs. Maroni like this, afraid of her husband that is, sitting there like a frightened child. Mama never felt that way. Mama wasn't afraid of anybody, least of all Papa. So she sat on the footstool and tried to reassure Mrs. Maroni that everything was going to be all right.

The men came back, sweating and laughing, and Mr. Maroni never said a word. If he noticed anything, he kept it to himself.

All in all, you'd have to say, Mama was a real classy lady that special autumn day with the Satsuma dishes and Tayste Raisin Cake and taking care of Mrs. Angela Maroni like she was a lost cat.

Maybe Mama doesn't know it, or maybe Mama doesn't come right out and talk about it, but there is still that dark shadow that follows her around: never going to school to learn how ro read and write, and whenever she has to sign her name to anything, how she presses her lips together so tight you can't hear her breathe, and then how, slowly, she picks up the pen and carefully, very carefully, makes a large X.

# Well, Maybe

Sometimes you look forward to things for years and years and then they change. They're not the same at all. Sometimes you know why and sometimes you don't. I know why I don't want to go up to Nanny Goat Hill tonight, to the St. Rocco Feast. Peter will be there, just as he has been every year since I was eight.

But this year was going to be different. Because I kept remembering last year. That night had been clear and warm, the street fair lit up by strings of lightbulbs swinging from one food stand to another. On First Avenue, a loud band played Italian folk songs. And everywhere you looked, small kids ran around waving balloons and furry monkeys on a stick.

My sister, Annie, dropped me off and said she would pick me up later.

I looked for Peter in the crowd, and then I saw him leaning up against the bandstand eating a hot dog. It seemed so important to me that he be there. Even if only to say hello, or to tease me about growing up.

"You didn't come up here alone, did you?" he asked

"No, I came with Annie, but she's with Michael." I said.

"I'm waiting for someone," he said, "but...I have some time, feel like walking around?"

I did.

I wondered if he still remembered that day in April when

he and his best friend Ray came to the house in Peter's new car, bright yellow with a rumble seat and a convertible hood. Really it was an old car, but it was Peter's first car and all he could afford. I remembered how I was getting ready to go to a novena at church when I heard the car's horn. Peter was at the wheel, smiling.

"Want to go for a ride?" he asked.

"You could take me up to church," I said. And then I heard Ray's voice. "Robbing the cradle, aren't you Peter?" Peter had looked embarrassed and I tried to act as though I hadn't heard.

As long as I had known Peter, we could kid around and talk and talk about everything and nothing, but suddenly after Ray's remark, I was uncomfortable, and even if I thought of something to say, the words just seemed to get lost somewhere between my brain and my tongue. I felt so stupid that day, and hoped Peter wouldn't notice. He didn't seem to. He had been quiet himself.

So, there we were, walking around the fair again. Peter jolted me out of my reverie.

"Want to sit awhile, Maria? Oh, sorry about that, kid. You're grown up now. You like to be called 'Midge' "

We had come to the end of a line of booths, with games and hawkers selling Italian ices. A grassy knoll overlooked rooftops and chimneys dotted here and there along dirt roads curving out of town.

The grass was cool, and it was nice, sitting there close to Peter watching the car lights pass by below like a parade of fireflies. After a while Peter said, "School will be starting up soon, are you glad?"

"Mmm, sort of, I guess. Summer is getting kind of boring." We just sat there, staring out at at the dark.

"I'm meeting Connie, you know Connie Merkle?"

"Yes," I said. "Is she your girlfriend?"

"I don't know," Peter said. He leaned over and tapped the tip of my nose and smiled. "C'mon, we better get back. Annie will be looking for you, and I don't want Connie to think I stood her up."

Just before we reached the spot where Connie was waiting, Peter said, "Wish you were all grown up, kid." Then he bent over and kissed me, a soft, quick kiss, but I felt like there were fireworks shooting off all around me.

Connie noticed us and walked over, her blonde hair bobbing on her shoulders, and she grabbed Peter's arm.

"I thought you stood me up," she pouted right in his face, and then she looked at me. "I didn't know you were with one of the kids from the neighborhood."

Connie was a splash of cold water, but I guess Ray didn't have to worry about Peter "robbing the cradle." Connie had already graduated from high school.

Sometime during this past year, Annie told me Peter and Connie were engaged. But Annie had to be wrong. Peter couldn't marry Connie. He is supposed to marry me when I grow up.

I kept waiting for Annie to tell me they had set a wedding date, but they were still just engaged.

Well, I guess Connie won't have to worry about the neighborhood kid this year, unless, maybe...

I looked at myself in the full-length mirror that hung on my bedroom door. I had grown taller and filled out since last summer. My black hair I used to wear short now fell over my shoulders in soft waves. Would Peter notice tonight at the St. Rocco Feast?

Maybe if I was pretty like Connie? I really wish I was pretty, but...I suppose you could say I'm nice looking, maybe even cute. Phil Costello liked me last winter, and we dated every Saturday night. We'd go to a movie in New York City and then have something to eat at Child's restaurant. Only one problem. When Phil dropped me off at the kitchen door, he always expected a goodnight kiss—and maybe it's me, but I really don't like kissing someone I'm not crazy about. So I decided to tell Phil I couldn't go out with him anymore. He felt bad, and I missed a lot of good movies, but I felt better about it.

One Saturday night while I was still going out with Phil, we met Peter and Connie on the bus to New York City. Phil had his arm around me, and we were sitting close. Peter looked at me without even smiling or anything and then sat down with Connie. I think I will always look for Peter, no matter who I date.

I remember the first day I met him. He and his mother had

walked down through the path in the woods from Nanny Goat Hill and came out on the street where I was making mud pies. I was eight and Peter was thirteen. He stood in front of me in a pair of baggy overalls and a plaid shirt, with his bright-red, curly hair sticking out all over his head.

I picked up a handful of the soft dirt and threw it at him.

"Hey, whatcha do that for, kid?" he yelled. It was the only way I could tell him I liked him. After that, Peter and his mother came to visit often. My mother and Peter's mother had just met, and now they were good friends. So, of course, the next time he came he said, "Are you going to throw dirt at me again, kid?"

"No," I said, "I did that already." And even though I was only eight, Peter didn't seem to mind spending time with me talking, or balancing on the metal pipe fence on the side of the house pretending we were tight rope walkers, or just hanging around.

One year, Peter helped me learn my lines for the Christmas play. He thought the play was sappy, but I had the leading part, so he tried to be serious about it.

Does he remember?

Maybe tonight, he will.

We'll find a spot on the grassy knoll and maybe Peter will put his arm around my shoulder and maybe he'll whisper, "The night I saw you and Phil on the bus, I realized how much you meant to me. I had a lousy time that night. Are you still seeing Phil?"

And then I'll say, "No, I'm not dating anyone. Are you still engaged?"

Maybe he'll say, "No. I'm waiting for you."

"I'm seventeen now," I'll say. Maybe, he'll look at me and smile. "You're growing up all right."

We won't talk about it anymore. We'll know. Just as we both knew the day he walked out of the woods with his red hair blowing every which way and I threw dirt at him, that one day... well, maybe.

# Kissing

The subway train from Broadway and Nassau to 168th Street rocked back and forth and the steady clickety-clack of the train over the rails was like a lullaby. I drifted into a reverie, my mind wandering beyond the subway train, and I began to think about my first kiss. And my second kiss. And all the kisses that came after. Well, perhaps not all the kisses, but the ones I really remember, *really remember*, 'cause either they were different in a special way, or scary, or I guess I could just pull them out of my memory without any effort at all. I guess what made kisses creep into my mind was Marcus, because kissing Marcus wasn't like any of those I ever did before.

Kissing, it seems, just sort of grows with you, like your toes and your ears and other parts of your body. It's something you notice—like mothers kissing babies and children, and hiding so you don't have to kiss aunts and uncles you don't like. Then at different ages, suddenly it becomes this embarrassing game that everybody wants to play, but they don't know why. And it's fun, because it's a secret game.

We were ten and eleven. I was eleven and Billy was ten and my younger brother's best friend. One afternoon, we were playing on the side of my house that faces the field, when Billy, who was standing close to me, leaned over and put his lips on mine. For just a second, but it seemed like at least as long as it took me to win a game of Hopscotch. His lips were small and soft and cool and the whole thing felt more like licking an ice cream cone.

"Now you're my girlfriend," he said. "You're the first girl I ever kissed."

Well, even if it was the first kiss I ever had from a boy, I didn't like hearing I was now his girlfriend, especially since he was younger than me and my kid brother's best friend.

"I am not," I said. Although when I thought about it again, it, the kiss was kinda nice, "You're younger than me."

Billy never kissed me again. And we went back to being just kids. There wasn't any embarrassment or silly feelings between us. It was as though it never happened.

But there were a lot of boys in the neighborhood and we played together in the open field, Johnny-Ride-the-Pony, Jackknives, Underleg, Marbles, and Hide-and-Seek. One of our favorite hiding places was the high grass. Sammy DeMario liked the high grass, too, and one day I thought I was safe, when along crawled Sammy toward me. And before I know it, he pushed his lips against mine till I thought I was going to swallow my teeth. "Wow, boy, that was great!" he whispered. Just as he was about to push his lips on mine again, I hauled off and socked him in the nose.

"You're a jerk, Sammy DeMario, and don't you ever do that again." I got up and ran out of the high grass and could have cared less if I got tagged. Sammy DeMario kissed me. It felt like I just fell in a mud puddle. I wiped my mouth with my sleeve and spit.

After that none of the girls hid in the high grass unless there was always someone else with them, and word got around that Sammy DeMario had "hand trouble" and that was worse than kissing, 'cause it meant you could have a baby with Sammy DeMario, or so we thought at the time, and nobody wanted to live with the DeMarios in that small house where all the grown up DeMarios were short and ate macaroni every night.

Well, there were a lot of kisses since then, mostly at birthday parties where we played Spin-the-Bottle and Post Office. The kisses were more like pecks, short and matter of fact. They never lasted longer than it took to turn a light on and off. Still, we girls talked about them, giggling and trying to decide who was the best kisser, but we weren't talking about the actual real kisses, we were really dreaming out loud. Actually, what did we know about kissing and what was good or bad or nice. But as we got older, something happened we weren't aware of at first, but it didn't take us too long to figure it out. Well, almost.

One afternoon, I sold my last school bus ticket to another kid for five cents so I could add it to the twenty-cents I had already saved from my lunch money to buy a pair of silk stockings at Woolworth's. It meant I would only have one ticket left for one bus ride. I had to take two buses home from high school, so now I would have to walk up the long hill. I'd done it before, and I knew it took time. It wasn't any big deal.

I was halfway up the hill when this old pick-up stopped, and this voice says, "Hey, Midge, want a ride home?"

It was Buddy, my cousin's brother-in-law. He was all right, but not a boy I would date. First of all, he was 19, and to me, that was too old. He said, ain't a lot, and once I asked him if he liked to read and he said, "I ain't interested in readin'. I got more important things to do."

The hill that day seemed twice as long and twice as steep. "All right," I said. I got in the truck, and when we got to the top of the hill, Buddy took a left-hand turn that went back to the old cemetery.

"Hey, Buddy" I said, "why are we going back to the cemetery?" Although, I was beginning to catch on. The old cemetery was a pretty lonely place, some people even called it Lover's Lane. But hardly any people ever visited the graves. Seems like people just forgot all about the dead who were buried there. Probably because there weren't any relatives left to visit them.

"If you don't take me home, Buddy, I'm walking." But before I could open the door, Buddy grabbed me and kissed me. Only it wasn't a normal kiss, the kind I knew about.

At first, I tried to figure out what was different, then I felt something odd, that wasn't lips. Oh, my God, it was his tongue. Buddy was "French kissing" me. Ugh, ugh, ugh! I pulled away. Buddy was laughing, and I could see one of his front teeth was missing. I was getting "French kissed" by a boy who had a front tooth missing. Ugh!

"I'm walking home, Buddy Lynch, and don't you ever do that again." But I didn't get out of the truck right off.

"Well," he looked at me and laughed, "I thought you might enjoy a grown-up kiss for once. Anytime you want another one, just let me know." He started up the truck, and we drove the rest of the way home, in silence. But he had a smile on his face.

I think that was the beginning, you know, like I said, that there was more to kissing than I ever thought. I had to admit that Buddy's kiss had a funny effect on me. Hard to catch the feeling and put it into words, but it was different.

At about the same time, a lot of the girls in town were crazy about Mark Morrissey and they all wished he would ask them out or give them a ride in his convertible. Not many of the boys had cars much less a convertible. And a boy with a car, wow! Driving down Main Street in a car with a boy, you had it made. So, I was flattered the evening Mark came to the house and asked if I'd like to go for a ride. Would I? Yes! My mother said, "Get home early," and Mark said we would. I sort of knew he'd try something, he had such a reputation for being "fast." But I thought I could handle him. He couldn't have been any worse than Buddy. I was wrong. I discovered that when Mark Morrissey was looking for a good time, he didn't take "no" for an answer. Dopey me!

It was getting dark, and Mark headed for the cemetery where it seemed darker than ever. He stopped the car and sprang at me like a cat at a mouse. I might have thought it was fun if we were playing Post Office, but out there in the dark cemetery, I suddenly felt like I was in trouble. I managed to open the door and I jumped out and slammed the door behind me. He laughed and called out, "Okay, you can walk home or give in." The darkness fell all around me, and it was spooky. I looked around. Row after row of gravestones lined up like sentries on both sides of the road. But I wasn't getting back in the car.

I started to walk up the road toward the main street. Mark followed me in the car. Just as we got to the gate that opened out onto the main road, he shouted, "OK. You win. I'll take you home."

But I wasn't sure he was telling the truth and I said, "No thanks, I'll get home myself."

He followed me slowly up the road.

"You don't believe me?" he asked.

"No," I said, "you're a creep!" That's when he hit the accelerator and went flying down the road. I felt like crying, and I didn't know what I would tell my mother. She would be madder than my stepfather gets when he runs out of wood for the furnace on a cold winter day. I was busy thinking up excuses when Mark pulled up again and stopped the car.

"Wait a minute," he said, "will you?" I stopped but kept a good distance from the car.

"I'll take you home, and I promise I won't try anything. Honest, I really mean it."

Somehow I knew he meant it, so I got in the car and he drove me home. And that was the last time I had anything to do with Mark Morrissey. I only wished I had a chance to see how he kissed.

Then there was Raymond. He was really nice and fun. His best friend, Keith had an old car with a rumble seat and dated my best friend, Sally. So on Saturday nights when the weather was warm, we would go for a ride. Raymond and I sat in the rumble seat and all the way from home to Bear Mountain, we would kiss and laugh and poke each other and kiss and laugh. Sometimes we stopped for ice cream, but mostly we just took the long ride to Bear Mountain and kissed and laughed. Kissing Raymond was sweet, just nice, soft and warm kissing. But then the kisses changed and we didn't laugh as much 'cause the kisses were longer. Were these the kind of kisses I read about in *Modern Love Stories* and *True Confessions*, where the girl heard heavenly music off somewhere before she melted away?

I guess Raymond was more serious about all that, but I wasn't, so after a while we stopped going for rides.

Just before Marcus, there was a young boy I dated, John, who couldn't make up his mind if he wanted to be a priest or just a guy. But we went together all summer after we graduated from high school. By then John had made up his mind about who he was, and he decided just being a good catholic was enough to save his soul.

Just because it's the way we do things, kissing was very important that summer. But looking back, getting to the kiss always seemed a little embarrassing, awkward, like it was still a sin or something. Or it was so important that if you sneezed while you were kissing, that was the end of the romance. Sometimes I just wished we could have talked or didn't have to say a word. Just sit there thinking our own thoughts. But the conversation always got back to us and how we were feeling, and so I repeated a lot of things I read in *True Confessions* that sounded romantic, and it worked.

John didn't have a car, so on those nights when we had a date, we either took a walk in the neighborhood or stayed at home. If my mother had gone to the local movie house on a night they were giving out another dish she could add to the collection of Satsuma dinnerware she was making, we would lie down on the couch together and John eventually would pull me close to him and whisper in my ear, "If we were in a house with just one bed, we would sleep together."

And I would say, "No, we wouldn't," and he would pull me closer to him and say, "Yes, we would."

And in between we would kiss. On nights when my mother was home, we sat on the couch. We played and kissed that way all summer until September, and then John went to Panama to work for three months. He asked me if I would wait for him to come home, and I promised I would. But I didn't.

I took a job running the billing machine with a nut, bolt, and screw company that had their office in New York City. Marcus was the person who prepared the bills, and I ran the machine. Marcus wasn't handsome, he was just nice looking. Not tall, about five-feet-eight-inches. Not fat, but not skinny. Blonde hair and brown eyes. After work, Marcus went to Cooper Union and took night classes in architecture.

Getting to know Marcus was easy. He was so easy to talk to, and when I made a mistake, he never criticized me: he just showed me what I did wrong and it was over. I could stumble over a word or do something stupid, and it was as though he never noticed. Working with Marcus was more than fun. I couldn't wait to get to work. After a while, he asked me if I wanted to keep him company after work when he walked to the subway station to get his train. So I did, only after we got there, Marcus offered to walk me back to my subway station, so I wouldn't be all alone on the city street. We laughed about that, and every night we joked about who was going to do the walking. If I walked him to his train, he always walked me back to mine, and we thought it was pretty funny. Everything we did together was just as though it was part of both of us, that we had been planned to fit somewhere ahead of time, 'cause it never seemed to be anything but the most natural thing in the world, just like waking up and going to sleep.

One day Marcus said, "How about going up to 42nd Street tonight after work? We can have supper at Childs and see a movie?" So we went to Childs first, and then we went to see *How Green Was My Valley*, and Marcus put his arm around me in the darkened theater and that was just fine. After the movie, we walked leisurely to the subway station and waited for my train.

We were standing close together and Marcus kissed me. For the first time. A short kiss. We looked at each other and smiled, and he kissed me again, this time a longer kiss. I could hear the train pulling out of the station, but I didn't care and we kissed again.

I wasn't melting into a puddle or anything like that, but I think I finally knew what that magazine story meant about heavenly music. They had it a little wrong, though, 'cause I didn't hear the music, but I felt something, like what Billy must have felt that day we were ten and eleven and he leaned over and kissed me. I think it must have been the same kind of shove.

# The Atheist

Molly looked confused, like a big question mark was hanging over her head. Her round eyes shuttled back and forth from one face to another.

"Well, I think my mother said we're atheists."

That's what she said—"I think we're atheists."

We all turned and stared at each other with this empty kind of look. I mean, what do you say after getting hit with a sacrilege like that?

It had been such a nice summer day. Molly, the new girl in the neighborhood, had walked over and joined me, my sister, Annie, my cousin Melia, and Lucy, a friend from down the road, on my front stoop, just sitting there talking. Overhead, branches from a cherry tree spread out like an umbrella, and it seemed so comfortable, like we were in a special place, not sitting on the stoop.

One of us—I don't remember who—brought up movie stars and which star we wanted to be like when we grew up, and then Melia wondered out loud if we should cut our hair short so we didn't have to put it up every night in curlers. We weren't about to stretch out one subject for long, so words just tumbled out of our mouths about menstrual periods and pimples and kissing boys, and pretty soon we slowed down and drifted back to remembering the day we made our First Holy Communions.

We had reached the age of reason, Sister Mulvena said. Of course, receiving the host was all wrapped up in holiness and should have been the main event in our life, but we thought of it as the day we got to wear a new white dress, white shoes, and a veil. Changing the little round host into the body and blood of Jesus, according to our catechism and Sister Mulvena—well, that could give you the shivers. Too hard to think about out loud. We decided to let that part of the sacrament stay in the catechism book, and we skipped right over to Confirmation. But we never got to talking about choosing a sponsor and vowing all kinds of holy things, because that's when Molly looked kind of stupid and asked, "Confirmation? What's Confirmation?"

So, my cousin Melia stuck out her chin and said, "You don't know what Confirmation is? What are you, a Protestant or something?"

That's when we all dropped dead, right after Melia asked her, "What are you?" and Molly said, "Well, I think my mother said we're atheists."

It was that word, atheist. One of those words that Sister would have talked about in catechism class first thing in the morning, and if she wrote atheist on the blackboard, she would have printed it in capital letters four feet high.

We just assumed when Molly moved into the gray house, the one we called the Wagner's place, that she was Catholic like the rest of us. I don't know if the other people who lived on our block thought about Molly's family being Catholic or whatever; they probably worried more about the new family being German like the Wagners. People whispered that the Wagners were Nazis, and after a while, they moved away. It wasn't a good time to be a German, what with Hitler and everything.

Anyway, none of us knew much about atheists except they didn't believe in God, which was bad enough, I guess, 'cause if you didn't believe in God, how could you believe in Jesus and the Holy Ghost? They all went together. Once in a while, though, I think about the Holy Ghost and wonder why, in pictures and the stained-glass window at church, they make him look like a pigeon. It's hard to think of a holy pigeon.

Still, I guess it was a good thing we found out Molly was an atheist. Now we wouldn't invite her to go to church with us on Saturday afternoon after we cleaned the house and took a bath. Why would an atheist want to sit around in church waiting for us to go to Confession and then hang around the cemetery reading gravestones?

But we didn't think about that stuff too much, and there was the long summer to get used to Molly before school started again.

So one day, just me and Molly were checking out our baseball cards to see if we had duplicates we could trade, and Molly gets real serious and says, "Now tell me the truth, Maria, the real, honest truth, like you're swearing on your Bible. Why do you believe there's a God?"

Well, you could have thrown me off the porch. I was just trying to decide if I wanted to keep both Babe Ruth cards or trade one for Lou Gehrig, and Molly, shuffling through her cards as though she were having any old conversation, asks me the most important question in my whole Catholic life.

"Why?"

For a minute, I hesitated. I didn't know which answer to give. Because Sister Mary Rose, the nun I had in fifth grade, said so. Or because I knew it was true.

"I just know it," I said, and hurried to give my answer some authority. "It says so in our Bible history book, and Sister says it's in the Bible."

"So what?"

Molly looked like Agnes Dougherty, one of my classmates who always thought she was right just 'cause she was the smartest kid in the fifth grade.

"The Bible isn't for real anyway," Molly said. "My mother said it was written by a bunch of men who didn't even know Jesus. And how could God and Jesus be the same?"

I felt like I had to defend God and everything a little better than I had been doing, but I didn't know what to say first. Then I began to say things, just anything that came into my head, and I started to feel like that martyr, St. Theresa, or some of those other guys who got their heads cut off.

"God and Jesus are the same. Get it? God is the father and Jesus is his son...only they are the same, you know, there's just one of them."

I was beginning to hear what I was saying, and I got a little confused, but I kept right on.

"...and Jesus died for our sins, and we receive him in Holy Communion. He's there, right there in the host, so I guess it's like we're receiving God."

Molly's face didn't change a wink. And what bothered me was, she didn't look as though she had to run around inside her head looking for answers and ways to show me I was wrong about God and everything.

I needed something big, something really important, like something that would keep her up at night, to really show her that atheists were all going to hell if they didn't wake up and believe in God.

"I can tell you a story, a story that Sister Rose told us about a lady, somebody just like an atheist, and what'll happen if you don't believe," I said.

Molly smiled, "Oh, I love stories. Is it long?"

"No," I said.

"Oh, nuts. I like long stories. Is it a fairy tale?"

"No," I said. "But it's a little bit scary. You really want to hear it?"

"Yup, yup!"

"Well," I began. "Once there was this woman. She was a really nice lady who wanted to see if the host really contained the body and blood of Jesus, like the Catholics say. Soooo . . . one Sunday morning, she went to Mass and received Communion . . ."

Molly was really listening. She wasn't fidgeting or twirling her hair.

"... and she didn't swallow the host. She kept it in her mouth 'til she got back to her pew. Then . . ." I waited, and very slowly, I said, " . . . she took the host out of her mouth and broke it in two pieces. And immediately, the church was flooded with blood!"

Molly opened her mouth. I looked right at her and gave my head a little nod like I was saying, "So there."

Molly closed her mouth and squinted her blue eyes. "Is that all?"

"The church was flooded with blood, Molly! Don't you get it? That's the story."

"I don't believe it, Maria. I think Sister Rose was just making it up, like a fairy tale."

Well, I couldn't believe Molly just said that. When Sister Rose told that story in class, I was so frightened, I could hardly receive Communion without worrying about where that host was in my mouth, bumping into my teeth and everything. And Molly thought it was a fairy tale.

Molly would probably go to hell, and there was nothing I could do about it. That made me feel bad, 'cause I really liked her. I didn't know why I liked her, but I didn't spend time trying to figure it out. Like, if she had been nasty and said mean things, or was a poor loser at hopscotch, or just a pain, I would have at least known why I didn't like her. So, I decided to stay friends anyway and maybe, I reasoned, we could convert her.

But, Molly must have thought about that story more than I realized, 'cause one day about a week later, she said, "Maria, you remember that story you told me about the woman who . . . Do you really believe that story you told me?"

"Sister Mary Rose wouldn't tell a lie."

"Could you do what that lady did?"

"Are you crazy? I would never do that!" I couldn't even look at her.

"You could see for yourself, Maria."

And God would probably strike me down dead or something. I didn't even want to talk about it.

But Molly had put some thoughts into my head that I had trouble forgetting. Every time I went to Communion for the rest of the summer, I was extra special careful not to let the host touch my teeth. And once I almost choked to death trying to get it down from the roof of my mouth without using my finger to move it.

All that stuff sat inside me like a bellyache you can get from eating too many bread-and-butter leaves in the woods back of the house. I guess I'm just one of those kids who likes to believe everything people tell them. Makes you feel good, like you're friends with the whole world, even when the stories are stupid, like my mother telling me that the little girl over on Catherine Street died that summer because she ate green pears. All us kids should have died at least a hundred times, then, if you could die from eating green pears.

So anyway, I couldn't stop thinking about the story I told Molly, and it kept coming up in my head sometimes when all I wanted to think about was nothing.

I kept remembering that Sister never said the woman was struck down by lightning or anything. And what about all those holy pictures that Sister handed out for good behavior and stuff, nice colored pictures of Jesus walking down a path and holding hands with some little kid? And I began to think he'd understand.

And I thought about what a good lesson it could be for Molly. She could stop being an atheist.

So one morning I woke up and decided I would do it. Just like that. Well, maybe I thought about it a long time through the summer, but anyway, that day I walked up to Molly's house to tell her.

She was eating toast and when I told her she started yelling, "Yeah! Yeah!" You'd think she just got an invitation to a birthday party with boys.

Molly must have seen the look on my face, not just being annoyed with her, but angry that she didn't understand how confused I was. She reached out and touched my arm.

"We don't have to, Maria," she said, raising her eyebrow. "But we can find out if it's for real." She tilted her head a little, almost like she was looking for an answer to a question.

She didn't look mean or anything. I thought she looked like she was sorry I was there. I didn't want to spend another minute thinking about it. So I told her our plans for how we would do it, as though we were a couple of explorers setting out on a mysterious journey.

"We'll go to church on Sunday," I said. "We'll have to attend the 11 o'clock Mass. The nuns won't be there. We can sit in one of the rear pews where we'll have more privacy."

Molly agreed.

My mother didn't think it was strange going to the late Mass. I did that whenever I got up too late for the 9 o'clock one.

The morning we decided to do it, I took one of my mother's special handkerchiefs, one of the ones edged in lace with embroidered flowers on one corner, and I put it into my white purse.

We sat in the last pew and had it all to ourselves. The late Mass was always poorly attended. More than once I wanted to get up and walk out, but I had to see what would happen.

So, I sang the hymns and knelt down and stood up and did all the things you have to do, until finally Father consecrated the host and people began to slip out of the pews and file slowly up to the altar railing to receive Communion.

I stood up and stepped out to join them. I kept thinking I should just get out of line and go back to my pew. But I kept right on walking down to where all the people were kneeling and receiving Communion and feeling good.

I knelt down and waited. When Father stood in front of me, I lifted my head slowly and Father had to wait for me to open my mouth wide enough for him to put the host on my tongue.

I folded my hands and stood up. It was hard to feel holy when all I could think about was what I was going to do. I walked real fast back to my seat and when I sat down, I quickly spit out the host into the handkerchief.

I sat there looking at it.

"Do it," Molly whispered.

"I will, I will."

I just kept looking at the host. Molly's hand came over and tried to pick it up.

"Stop!"

The man in the pew in front of us turned slightly and said, "Ssssssh!"

"I said I'll do it."

My teeth were clenched. I was so mad at Molly, but I guess that was what I needed, to get mad, really mad at Molly if I was going to do it.

My hand was shaking when I picked up the host. I closed my eyes and felt my fingers slowly break the wafer in two.

I waited.

There wasn't a sound. I waited for Molly to scream, but she didn't. No one else did, either.

I slowly opened my eyes and looked around the church to see what had happened. It was quiet except for the fans turning overhead. The monsignor was chanting in Latin at the altar. The statue of the Virgin Mary was still gently smiling, and Joseph, his statue was on the other side of the altar, was still standing there with his head bowed like he was looking for his shoes or something.

Candles flickered and the floorboards were waxed to a shine. Nothing had happened.

Why?

God knows everything, Sister said. Didn't he know I was going to . . . I couldn't even think it.

Molly had a big smile on her face.

"Whadda ya think, Maria?" I felt like smacking her, but I just sat there staring ahead.

Father left the altar with the altar boys, and people filed out of the pews and quietly walked out of the church.

"Let's go, Maria."

Molly stood up and waited for me to slide out of the pew. I pulled her down and said, "Wait!"

I always felt better in church after everybody left. That's when it's nice being alone, with nobody to get in your way. And there's still the smell left over from the incense burning in the round ball Father swings around after Mass, blessing everybody.

So we sat there a little while longer, and I felt small and strange, like I didn't know who I was and couldn't believe I had touched the host. I kept looking at my fingers, as though I expected them to be different or to have a mark on them, anything. Molly was squirming in the seat and getting impatient.

"Okay," I finally said. We walked slowly back to the heavy oak doors, and for just an instant, I hesitated opening the door and stepping out of the church. There was still this feeling that maybe something was going to happen. I thought maybe God wasn't finished with me yet.

But when we walked out onto the sidewalk, the morning was like any other morning after church. Cars were pulling away from the driveway and some people were just hanging around talking to each other.

Molly wanted to talk about what happened on the way home, but I couldn't. I was all mixed up between thinking about what I did and wondering if I had committed a mortal sin. I didn't want to hear myself or anyone else say a word.

When we got to my house, I said, "I don't ever want to talk about what happened in church today, ever again, Molly. Do you hear me? And you have to promise you won't say a word to anybody. You hear? Molly, you have to promise!"

Molly looked at me. "I don't see why we can't talk about it." The sound of her words felt like she had just stamped her foot.

"Molly, you can't! You understand. You just can't." I almost screamed.

She finally nodded her head up and down. "Ok, I promise, but I don't see why it should be such a big secret."

Of course she didn't. She's not Catholic. She's an atheist!

"'Cause I just said so, and you'll never understand what this means and how I can't ever receive Communion again, ever again, in my whole life."

I didn't even bother to tell her that I'd never confess what I did, and that meant every time I went to Confession it would be a bad Confession and another sin on my soul. And by the time I'm ready to die, my soul will probably have a million sins on it and I'll go straight to Purgatory, or maybe even hell, and have to think about what I did for ever and ever.

Molly never thought of that, did she? I had to think about not being friends with Molly, too, but that thought made me sad, 'cause I liked her.

So, Molly didn't bring it up again, although there were times when we just sat around kind of quiet, just thinking our own stuff, when she would slip me a look and I could tell she had to bite her tongue.

And I made bad Confessions. And the sins added up on my soul. I didn't receive Communion ever again, and that was very tricky not to get noticed. I had to get up late lots more times and just lie about it, which added sins on top of sins.

Before you know it, me and Molly graduated from grammar school. I went to St. Bridget's High, and Molly went to a private boarding school, so we didn't get to see each other too much anymore. We wrote letters every now and again, and whenever she came home on holidays, it seemed Molly left a little more of the Molly I knew back at her school.

I couldn't tell if Molly was still an atheist or not, 'cause we didn't talk about religion anymore. Boys and grades and parties and stuff were more fun.

And me. Well, after a while, I stopped worrying about that Sunday, but I must be superstitious or something like that. I still couldn't receive Communion.

Now high school is over and I'm looking forward to working in the big city. And Molly, she's going off to one of those Protestant lady colleges where I guess it doesn't matter if you're an atheist.

So, here I am, standing outside the white church with seventy-four other graduates from St. Bridget's High School, waiting to enter the church and attend the Baccalaureate Mass for graduating seniors.

I don't think anyone is thinking about receiving Communion or what it means, all the things we were taught and believed when we were kids. Being here is just part of the whole thing that happens when you finally get to graduate from high school, leaving friends and thinking we're ready to grow up, only now, hoping we know a little more.

I invited Molly to come to the Mass with my mother, and she thought it was a great idea. The experience would be good for her, she said. If she was thinking about the Communion thing, she never let it show, never said a word, like she promised years ago.

I never did tell her what I had done with the handkerchief, either. I will though.

I'll tell her that when I got home that day, I went straight up to the attic. I like the attic. It's quiet and smells of chamomile that my mother gathers in the field and ties in little bunches and hangs on the rafters to dry. That day, I had to find something to put the handkerchief in and a place where it could stay forever. Under the small windows that look out over the front yard, there was a box of junk, and sitting right on top was a flat Lucky Strike tin box. It was empty, so I carefully placed the handkerchief in the tin. It fit real nice. I pushed aside one of the trunks that stood where the ceiling begins to slope to the edge of the attic, and I slid the tin on the floor toward the back of the eaves, way back until it disappeared into the dark corner.

I thought I would never look at that handkerchief again, but just the other day, I guess with graduation happening and thinking about Molly coming to the Baccalaureate Mass, I wanted to see the handkerchief one more time. I'm not sure if what I was feeling was just curiosity or something else, something I couldn't even name.

No one was around the house, so I went up to the attic and pulled the tin out from under the eaves. A thin layer of dust dulled the Lucky Strike letters, but it was still intact. I opened the lid and carefully unfolded the handkerchief. Scattered around were some little bits of crumbs and a small smear of host still clinging to the handkerchief.

I stared at it. Just kept staring. I thought I might get the shivers again, but instead, I felt sad. So, I sat there a few minutes. I thought I should. It didn't seem right to just close the tin and put it back without sharing a little of my time.

Anyway, I won't be receiving Communion today. I told Sister I ate a cookie in the middle of the night. That I got hungry. She wasn't happy, but we all know the law: no eating after midnight, if you plan on receiving in the morning. I'll be sitting there alone, the only student dressed in my cap and gown, sitting in an empty pew, and I suppose people will wonder why, and maybe for a minute, they'll just think I'm a Protestant.

I'm not worried about committing another sin by lying to Sister about the cookie, either, because I made so many bad Confessions not telling the priest what I did that morning, one more sin won't matter. I'm not even worried about the venial sins on my soul, that is, if I have one.

I've been thinking about that a lot, too, lately.

I turned around to see if I could pick out Molly in the crowd of parents and friends sitting in the rear pews. She's sitting next to my mother and another woman who's wiping her eyes with a handkerchief. Some people cry at all kinds of ceremonies.

Molly doesn't look sad or happy. I guess she's just getting experience, like she said. One day soon, I think, we'll sit down, look back, and talk about that morning. Because we have to.

Maybe, we'll even laugh a little, like friends.

# The Billing Clerk

Astiff breeze, lightly touched with the smell of the river down below, whipped up the narrow city street, I took in a deep breath.

I liked it.

I liked everything about the morning. Unfamiliar people rushing by, noisy cars and taxi cabs. There were even these moaning sounds of ship horns from the river.

I smiled. This wasn't Main Street, slow and familiar, in the small town where I lived all of my seventeen years. I was sure this city street was the world I had pictured and dreamed of when I was sitting in high school business class, listening to the tapping of keys on Royal typewriters.

I walked a little faster searching for the office of a nut and bolt company in one of the old weathered buildings that filed down both sides of the street all the way to the waterfront. An employment agency had sent me on an interview, and I didn't want to be late.

The buildings had almost run out and I was beginning to panic when I noticed the large gilt sign, Adam's Nut and Bolt Company, hanging on the side of a shabby two-story building with shuttered windows.

For just a few seconds I stood there, then quickly checked my silk stockings, made sure the seam that ran down the back of my leg was straight. I ran my hand over my hair, took out my compact, and examined my lipstick. Then I pushed open a heavy wooden door that had a small glass insert just above my eye level.

I stepped into a musty vestibule, dimly lit and rather small. A little disappointing. I guess I was expecting a large bustling business with people moving about, doing things. But in front of me were two staircases, one going up, marked "Office," and one going down, marked "Shipping."

I picked the staircase going up. At the top of the stairs, I stepped into a very large room with fewer people than I had imagined. Although, I didn't really know what to expect, how an office should look or even smell. On the other hand, I didn't expect the room to look as though it had been left over from the Revolution.

The walls were wood paneled and covered pipes crept along the ceiling. Seeping out from everywhere was this musty smell, probably trapped there forever, since all the windows were boarded up by those shutters on the outside of the building.

Large light bulbs covered with green metal shades hung from the ceiling, lighting the room and casting shadows over the typewriters, adding machines, and the men and women working at their desks.

From the minute I walked through the heavy door and entered the building, I had this odd feeling, as though I were living the first sentence in a novel: The young girl entered a world she knew nothing about.

No one seemed to notice me standing there. At one end of the room, an older woman sat at a desk surrounded by filing cabinets. She looked up and stared at me for a minute as though I were the usual visitor, and then went back to whatever she was doing. There was a steady hum and everyone at their desks seemed busy.

Along one wall, jackets, coats, and umbrellas hung limply on brass hooks, but there didn't seem to be any order to the arrangement of desks and worktables. I had no idea where I should go, so I walked over to one of the desks where a man sat with his head about six inches from a book he was reading. I hoped he was someone like a boss or a manager.

I stood there waiting for him to look up and notice me, but he didn't. Neither did anyone else seem to be interested in what I was doing there, as though everyone expected I would do what I came for and then leave.

After a few minutes, I cleared my throat, real loud.

You would have thought I dropped a bomb. The man looked up, startled, as though he had been sleeping. Before he had a chance to say a word—although he didn't look as though he were going to say or do anything, his eyes were still blank—I said, "The Acme Employment Agency sent me."

"Oh, yes, yes," he finally said, "About the billing job. Yes. Yes. Please." He rose and pointed to a chair, "Sit down, please."

I sat down and caught a glimpse of the book he was reading. He had closed it and on the cover it read, The Sun Is My Undoing. I wondered if it was like a Zane Grey novel. I could get lost in one of those, too.

He was tall and thin, and his body seemed to sag in a rumpled suit that looked as though he'd slept in it. I was surprised, too, that for a man who had to be about fifty, his hair was still dark with only a speck of gray around his ears. He wore glasses, which he immediately took off. When I first saw him, I thought he was older, but up close, his eyes seemed so much younger than his face. Must be a very good book, I decided, to turn off the world and not hear what was going on.

He caught me looking at the book. He put his hand on the cover and patted it.

"Yes," he said, "I was so involved in the book, I didn't hear you. But, let's see, you're here for the billing machine position. Now what did you say your name was?"

After we got through the preliminaries of name, age, school, and requirements to do the job, he said, "Do you want to be a billing clerk?"

I hesitated for just a minute. I really hated arithmetic, mathematics, anything that looked like a number, and he was asking me if I wanted to work in the bookkeeping department on a billing machine, typing out versions of one-to-ten all day.

"Yes," I said, and added without thinking, "But I hate arithmetic."

He seemed puzzled, but I turned and looked at the men and women busy at their bookkeeping machines and, before he had a chance to say anything, I said, "But if these people can do it, so can I."

He gave a short laugh.

"I like your attitude," he said. "Your independent spirit. The billing job is yours."

He smiled, and I thought he looked at me just a little too long and hard, you know, sort of taking me all in. I can't explain it, but I know how it made me feel. Like he had just touched me.

"I'll introduce you to Marcus. You'll be working with him." He called out to a boy about my age. "Marcus, I want you to meet the young lady who is going to be working with you on the billing machine. Miss Ferri."

"And by the way," he said, turning to me again, "I'm George Vandermeyer, vice president of the company."

Mr. Vandermeyer didn't seem to do much, I learned over the next month, except supervise the bookkeeping department and now and again, he would dictate a letter and I would type it up for his signature and that would be that. In between, he read that book, The Sun Is My Undoing.

Then one morning after I had finished one of those letters for him, he began to tell me that he had fired the pretty girl he recently hired to run one of the bookkeeping machines because she wasn't too bright. He felt bad, he said, but she just couldn't get the hang of it. I don't know why he told me that, 'cause it just made me feel bad for her and wonder if maybe there was something I didn't know.

Actually, he never talked to me much, except once in a while, he would close the book and call me over to just chat about how I was doing. But he liked to gossip a little, I think, 'cause he always had something to say about the people who worked there. Like the old woman who ran the filing department: She could be crabby, he said, but I shouldn't mind what she said whenever I wanted something in the files. She was the only one who knew how the filing system worked. She had been there since the business started, and she had put in the system. She never told anyone how it worked and they were all too busy to ask, so the years went by and now she was the only one who knew where to find anything. So they couldn't fire her. He laughed when he said that.

I didn't have any trouble with her, though. I was nice and polite when I needed something from the files, the way I was taught in the Catholic school business course.

"She likes you," Mr. Vandermeyer told me, and he didn't exactly smile even though the corners of his mouth turned up. He looked more like he was thinking something.

I liked working at the Adam's Nut and Bolt Company. The president's secretary, an older woman probably in her thirties, invited me to lunch lots of times. She was nice, told me lots of things about the company, like how her boss would get real mad at his brother, George—Mr. Vandermeyer—but couldn't fire him 'cause the two brothers had started out together and the family would be angry with him if he tried to. I really felt like I had been working there forever.

Then everybody started teasing me about Duncan. He worked downstairs in the shipping department and he would come up and walk around the room and everybody said he did that just to see me. Except Mr. Vandermeyer, who said Duncan wasn't getting paid to impress me, and he should realize that I wasn't interested in him.

Well, I never thought of Duncan as someone to date. He had to be at least twenty-two or twenty-three, and I never dated anyone that old before. He was tall and thin, and he had a long face and wore glasses. He acted so grown up. I think the True Story Magazine would have called him, "sophisticated" in one of their love stories. So when he asked me to have lunch with him one day, I said, "Okay." Why not? Might be fun to date someone I never would have met in the small town where I grew up.

We went to a little restaurant close by and sat at a table with a white tablecloth and a vase of flowers. We sat there and didn't say a word. I couldn't think of anything to say, and Duncan didn't help, either. I guess it was because he was older and I didn't know him and he was so serious, looking at me through those glasses. I thought how different a date with one of the boys from my neighborhood would be. No one would be grasping for words or leaving minutes of time just silent. We'd talk so much we might even forget to eat while the food was warm. We'd know things, together.

A waitress came, and Duncan and I ordered food and waited. Well, it wasn't long before I started squirming in the chair. Then I bent down and scratched my ankle. Then I straightened my sweater over my skirt, and by that time, I was doing things absentmindedly. Just before I began to tie my napkin into a knot, the food came. We ate without saying a word to each other, which was easier—eating gave us something else to do than just sit there feeling like we'd like to disappear. Then we walked back to the office, and I said, "Thank you."

I went up to the office, and he went down to the shipping department. After that Duncan didn't visit the office anymore, so nobody teased me about him and Mr. Vandermeyer seemed real pleased and had this odd look on his face, when he stopped by my machine one morning and said, "Of course, you realize, Duncan is just a foolish boy."

I really didn't care anymore. I'd just have to do some more thinking about sophisticated older boys. Anyway Marcus, my partner at the billing machine, was much more fun, and we always had something to say to each other.

Sometimes Mr. Vandermeyer would look over at us like he thought we talked too much, but he didn't say anything. Mostly Mr. Vandermeyer read his book, leaning over his desk and not seeming to know what was going on in the bookkeeping department.

I decided one Saturday after I left the office for the day—we just worked a half day on Saturday—to stop in at my local library and see if I could get that book and maybe browse through it and see why Mr. Vandermeyer was so attached to it.

The librarian, Miss Nardone—a woman who had been there since I was in grade school and had only one look on her face, unfriendly—gave me a very disapproving look when I asked if she had the book, as though I had just asked for something illegal. She gave it to me and asked if I were taking it out, but I told her I just wanted to look through it, read a little of it here and there.

Then she looked at me as though I were some kind of pervert.

The first thing I noticed was the number of pages, over a thousand. A very thick book. And the print was small. No wonder it was taking Mr. Vandermeyer so long getting through it. It wasn't like a Zane Grey book. It just went on and on about Cuba and this guy Matthew Flood, and a family of slave traders, and wars, and slaves in chains, and men who had mistresses and wives at the same time and "lusted" a lot.

I was beginning to think that book wasn't a very good book for Mr. Vandermeyer to be reading in the bookkeeping department every day. Then one afternoon he called me over to his desk.

"Tonight, I want you to stay and get some extra billing done."

I had never worked overtime, but I guessed it was not unusual.

At five when everyone left for the day, they turned off all the lights in the other departments, and the only light was the one over my machine and the light over Mr. Vandermeyer's desk, so most of the room was in shadows, and the light over my machine and his desk seemed so dim and pale. A wind had begun to blow up from the river not too far from the Nut and Bolt building, and every now and again the old rafters creaked, and sometimes it almost felt as though the building was shaking.

I worked at my machine thinking about the amount of work Mr. Vandermeyer expected me to do. Whenever I turned around to see what he was doing, I would catch him looking at me. Then he would quickly turn to his book.

We had been working about an hour when he said, "Miss Ferri, I thought I heard something up in the loft. Did you hear that noise?" He caught me by surprise with that word loft. It was an old building, probably a hundred years old or more, so I guess it could have a loft.

"No," I said. "I didn't hear anything."

"Sounds like chains, like someone dragging chains on the floor?"

I didn't turn around and look at Mr. Vandermeyer, but from the sound of his voice, I could almost see him sitting there under the dim light with the book opened in front of him, his face looking old but oddly young under the pale light and his eyes dark and half closed with an unfamiliar look on his face.

He was getting spooky.

I kept right on working and said, "It's just the wind."

But I was thinking it was probably all about that book, with all that stuff about slaves and chains. Where else would he get such an idea? If he thought I was going up into that loft to look for ghosts and I don't know what else, I was not. If he wanted to play games, he could play by himself.

Just thinking about it made me type faster, get those bills done. A while later, he said, "Ssssh! Listen, I hear them again,"

This time Mr. Vandermeyer whispered, "I think we should investigate what's going on up there. Come on, let's go up and see."

His voice was low and sounded like someone trying to coax a cat out from under the couch or something. I was convinced it was that book. One thousand pages of small print and all that stuff about "delivering his nights to orgies..." That's exactly what some of the small print had said when I browsed through it at the library.

"Don't you think we should go up to the loft and investigate those noises?"

His voice was serious, as though he were giving me a job to do and expected me to carry out his instructions. I turned around and saw that he was now standing up. Whatever he had in mind, I didn't wait to find out. I stood up and turned around and looked straight at him, just as sure as I did the day I faced him and said I hated arithmetic.

"No, I don't. I'm finished, and I'm going home."

We were standing there now, perfectly still, facing each other, and I don't know what happened, but he looked surprised and his eyes widened. Then just as fast, they turned strangely vacant as though he had lost his place. He didn't say a word. He just stood there, looking at me.

I didn't wait for him to explain what was happening. I put the bills neatly aside for the morning, turned off my machine, walked over and picked up my coat hanging on the wall.

I didn't turn back. I hurried down the stairs to the lobby, now lighted only by a street lamp from out on the city street, the glow coming through the small window in the door.

I was about to open the door and step out onto the sidewalk when I heard Mr. Vandermeyer call out. "Miss Ferri, wait."

His voice sounded flat. There was a pause and then he said, "I'll walk you to the subway. This isn't a good neighborhood for young girls to be alone this time of night."

I would rather have walked to the station by myself, but I waited. Mr. Vandermeyer kept his head down when he stepped out of the building. He said nothing and began to walk ahead of me, his shoulders hunched under a black chesterfield coat. He never turned to see if I was following him, and we didn't say a word to each other.

When we got down to the station platform, he distanced himself from me and stood quietly facing the tracks. There were a few other commuters waiting for the train, so I felt more comfortable. When the train finally fumed out of the tunnel and came to a hissing stop, I moved toward the doors that were slowly opening and stepped into one of the cars. Mr. Vandermeyer stood there for a few minutes and then walked away towards the stairs.

The next morning, I reluctantly got up and went to work. Somehow, things didn't feel the same. The hum hadn't changed. But Mr. Vandermeyer wasn't at his desk, and the top had been cleaned of his personal belongings. Marcus was the first to tell me the news, which I later learned had puzzled the other employees, especially the president's secretary.

"He never came in," she said. "He phoned his brother; said he needed a vacation and didn't know when he'd be back. He's never done anything like that."

I didn't tell her about the night before. When I stopped to think about it, I figured Mr. Vandermeyer, for the past month, wasn't at his desk working out things about bookkeeping and nuts and bolts. He was with the hero of his book, Mathew Flood, probably dreaming through the pages about adventures he never knew and might never know. And maybe he wasn't ready to come home.

As for me, well, I guess I was learning real fast about this new sophisticated world. I don't know if I would discover anything new about Mr. Vandermeyer if I read *The Sun Is My Undoing*, but I can wait. And whatever Mr. Vandermeyer learns on his vacation, well, I seriously think he ought to at least try to take his mind off some things, and maybe it would help if he brought along a couple of real good Zane Grey novels.

# The Pout

Katy Ryan wore a winter white dress to the Christmas party that year in 1941, short, just above the knees, and cinched at the waist with a bright red belt that matched her shoes, not to mention her lips, also shaded in brilliant red. Her Celtic black hair she wore long and straight.

She was trying to look as though she were part of the holiday festivities standing with some of the other typists at a refreshment table set up for the employees. But even from where I sat at my desk, I could see her lips drawn into a pout, one of those habits I guess people hang on to even after they grow up 'cause it just gets to be part of them. After hanging around with Katy for the past six months—we were both hired on at the bank at the same time—I got to understand just how her habit worked. If she scowled and pursed her lips for just about a half a minute or so, she was annoyed with something unimportant. But if she squinted and wrinkled her brow and pouted for at least a half a day, then she was really mad about something that she wouldn't talk about and she might not even eat lunch.

This pout was different, real serious, almost sad, as though she were on the verge of tears.

"Something's bothering Katy today," I heard Jane, my other best friend, whisper over my shoulder.

Jane stood in back of my chair, looking over at Katy.

"Look at her, she's gonna bust out crying any minute. I think maybe we should go over and see what's wrong."

By the time we got to Katy, tears were smudging her mascara. When we suggested getting away from the party to talk, maybe up to the small lounge in the Ladies restroom, she looked relieved.

"I'd like that," she said. "I have something I want to talk about, not that I really want to, but I think this is a good time."

I'm pretty sure both Jane and I had the same thought: Bob—Lt. Robert Morrissey, Katy's boyfriend—had to be responsible for taking the holiday out of Katy's day. It had to be Bob, 'cause they'd been going steady for a year, and for weeks Katy had been dreading the day Bob would get transferred to England, now that we were in the war with Germany.

It didn't take long for Katy to burden us with why she was so unhappy.

"Well, last night Bob told me he was being shipped out today, to England, you know. And I cried, I mean, I couldn't stop. Even though I knew this day was coming..." Katy wiped her eyes. "So, we went back to his apartment just to be alone, and we had some wine, and one thing led to another, and before you know it, I think Bob and me...we...we...went too far last night."

She looked embarrassed and we were totally taken by surprise. I mean, we expected it had something to do with Bob, but this... Oh, my!

But it was just the kind of material Jane and I needed to feed our imagination. And it did!

The minute we got back to our desks, we tried to put two and two together.

"It still depends on 'how far,' Jane. I mean, you know, just... you know..."

I had trouble explaining "how far." I wasn't sure I knew exactly when you went too far. I suspected Jane knew exactly what Katy meant, and I just wished I did.

What was it really like, I wondered? I couldn't think of one relationship with a boy that made me feel as though I wanted to go further than hugging and kissing and feeling light-headed and warm.

"She probably should just go to Confession and quick," Jane said. That meant it was bad, really bad, and I didn't know what to think.

"Should we ask her?"

I'm not sure I meant to say that, or was I just making conversation? I was so nervous, 'cause I never came so close to anything like this before. I knew about all the other mortal sins, some of them were pretty bad, but I didn't worry about them, 'cause I didn't plan on killing anybody or something terrible like that. The most penance I ever got in my whole life was ten Hail Marys. Cursing and thinking bad thoughts was safe enough. If you couldn't get to Confession all you had to say was "I'm sorry"—that's what they call "a firm act of contrition"—and God heard you, and it was forgiven.

But this other stuff. Boy!

"So, should we ask her?" I said again.

Jane made a face. "I don't think so. We better just wait and see if she wants to say anything more to us."

"If it's that bad, what can we say, anyway?"

Jane didn't answer right off. Then, "We'll wait and see."

About a half hour from quitting time, Katy asked us if we'd go with her to a nearby church after work. She wanted to go to Confession, she said. She didn't want another day to pass.

"Of course we will," Jane said.

Later, the three of us walked to the church, open late to accommodate workers in the area. A sprinkling of people were inside, some standing near the confessional, others kneeling in the pews, and a few kneeling at the altar, probably saying their penances.

I guess I should have been thinking more about Katy and how sad she felt, but all I could think of was, what did she do? I was sure Jane had it on her mind, too.

Katy joined the others standing in line outside the confessional, and Jane and I walked down to a pew close to the altar railing. The minute we sat down, Jane bent over and said, "Wonder what kind of a penance the priest will give her. We could be here a long time, if..." Jane raised her eyebrows.

I didn't say anything, I just tried on a little smile so everything wouldn't seem so gloomy even with all the Christmas decorations.

The number of people waiting for Confession got smaller, and when I looked around to see where Katy was in line, she was gone. She was in the confessional already. I have to admit, I was excited. I poked Jane, who was concentrating on her rosary beads.

"She's talking to the priest right now," I said.

Jane turned around. "No, she's coming down the aisle now."

Jane's voice rose a bit in the quiet church, and the sound of Katy's high heels echoed like the steady rap on a drum.

We waited for the sound of her heels to reach our pew. Jane was sitting near the aisle, so when Katy was alongside us, Jane reached out and grabbed her coat. Katy stopped.

"Is your penance long?" Jane asked.

Katy bent down and whispered in Jane's ear and then continued down the aisle to the altar rail. I noticed the pout was gone.

"Well, what's the penance?"

Jane just looked at me as though she had just heard something she didn't expect to hear. She whispered, "Ten Hail Marys."

I could tell Jane was disappointed.

# Laughing Girl

Her mother wanted a good life for Midge. But it had to include the telephone company and six pairs of silk stockings.

"But, Midgie," her mother would say in a voice that sounded like she was singing a lullaby. "Think about it, the telephone company. Right around the corner. Home for lunch. No carfare. And every Christmas the bookies in town give the girls six pairs of silk stockings. Silk stockings today, with a war going on and all the silk going into parachutes. All you have to do is give the bookies good service. Connect them to the right people."

All that summer after high school graduation, her mother's advice followed her around like a pet dog.

It wouldn't have done Midge a wink of good to tell her mother she dreamed of offices tucked away in some building high above the city streets, smelling of typewriter ribbons and Evening in Paris perfume, where she would meet people who didn't look like anybody she ever knew. Where people did things she didn't expect them to do, like join the Rosicrucians or something.

Her mother would never know why Midge wanted to meet new people who were different from anybody she already knew. It was probably as hard for her mother to understand as algebra was for Midge.

Some evenings, Midge would walk down to the Palisades where she could look out across the river at the skyscrapers crowding the city's skyline and, as though someone had cast a magic spell on her, she felt like a different person. Nobody seemed to understand why she had to work in New York City. Nobody. Especially her mother.

So, for the summer months, Midge found a temporary job with a local realtor who didn't sell too many houses, but he could afford to pay her $5 a week to answer the phone in case it rang. All day, she sat in a swivel chair in front of a rolltop desk piled high with Mr. Biamo's papers and gazed out the plate glass window at Main Street.

If Mary Contrini walked by, Midge could immediately give you the most important fact about her: she was the boss in the family. Or Tony Catelli, poor Tony, he stuttered and you had a headache before his words straightened out so he could let you know he had a headache. Or the three Kearney sisters who wore large-brimmed straw hats and walked side by side up Main Street every Sunday morning on their way to church, forcing anyone who tried to pass them into the gutter.  Midge knew everybody in her small town, even those who didn't want her to know them.

Every now and again that summer, when her mother thought about it, sometimes with a smile, she nagged. "Think about it. Silk stockings."

Sometime in September, Midge received a call from a large bank near Wall Street where she had filled out a job application. They had an opening for a typist in the Bond Department.

She started work the following week. She worked there for two months before she met Geraldine O'Malley.

But first she met Jane and Ruth who lived in Forest Hills and dressed in a lot of navy blue and wore trench coats and brown loafers. Both had light brown hair, soft like silken corn tassels, pulled back from their foreheads and clipped with tortoiseshell barrettes. Midge's black curly hair defied barrettes. No one who worked at the bank resembled anyone she knew from the small town in New Jersey where she had lived all her seventeen years.

Midge would tag along with Jane and Ruth, but she missed a lot of the conversation. Walking three abreast on the crowded sidewalks of Wall Street was impossible. Someone had to follow in back, and it was usually Midge. It didn't help that Midge was five feet tall and both Jane and Ruth were over five feet six.

But when the three of them went to lunch, Midge really had trouble with the conversation. More than just the span across the Hudson River separated them. Jane was Irish and Ruth was Irish, and they fit together like they were twins. They spent the entire lunch hour talking about Forest Hills, the Knights of Columbus, and Jane's father who was a lawyer on Wall Street. You could tell just listening to Ruth and Jane that probably no one yelled in their houses. There were just conversations. And they probably used cloth napkins every day at every meal, not just on Sunday.

Somehow, the St. Rocco Sodality and Grandpa playing the tuba in the band didn't quite have the ring of Forest Hills and Irish track stars.

All that changed when Gerry came to work at the bank, and Jane and Ruth were transferred. Midge didn't see them too often after that. She was relieved. Laughing with them all the time was exhausting.

Midge wanted to talk about things, serious things like Émile Zola. Midge was reading *Nana*, and even though she had wrapped it in brown paper so no one would know she was reading a racy book, she knew it was important and probably no one in her town was reading Émile Zola. Jane and Ruth didn't even seem to know that other people—and the radio, and the whole world—were talking about the war in Europe, priorities, and Civil Defense.

She soon discovered Gerry was different, too. The morning she walked into Midge's cage, everybody stopped working and watched Gerry sway into the room as though her entire body were drifting on air. She was tall, not heavy, and her short skirt outlined her body like a pencil drawing and all the men seemed to notice. She carried a black Chesterfield coat over her arm and, perched at a cocky angle on her thick auburn hair, she wore a black derby hat. Halfway through the room, she stopped and looked around. Midge thought she'd never seen such eyes before. They were green, dark and deep, like summer leaves.

"Hi," Gerry said and looked down at Midge.

Gerry's lips were full and petulant with front teeth too small for such a generous mouth. But, as Midge discovered, Gerry didn't smile a lot anyway, so she didn't have to worry about small teeth. She would outline her lips with a bright shade of lipstick applied so thick that, by the end of the day, after coffee breaks and lunch, lipstick smudged the corners of her mouth and a lot of it was on her front teeth.

Gerry had a lot of friends who worked around Wall Street. Once, when they all met at Nedicks for hot dogs and orange drinks, Gerry introduced them to Midge. They seemed so grownup, so sophisticated. They smoked. And they knew how to hold a cigarette. They even inhaled without getting dizzy and falling flat on their faces.

Listening to them talk about their boyfriends, Midge felt that somewhere she had lost a few years. She had never been serious enough with a boy to discuss her menstrual period, but they did that and more. Midge just wished she had a boyfriend.

But Gerry didn't have a steady boyfriend either, so there were no big discussions about being madly in love and what happened on dates.

Sometimes after work on warm evenings when the sounds of the streets seemed softer and the air was so sweet it made Midge feel like her face was smothered in a bouquet of lilacs, they would take the ferry over to Staten Island. Leaning on the railing, smelling the salt air mixed with the spray from the murky water, they never had to talk, though they sometimes dreamed aloud to each other.

"We could get an apartment in the Village and go to NYU at night."

Midge liked these times: she could tell Gerry anything, and Gerry never laughed at her.

"And we could take up psychology like Jim. Then we'd know what he was talking about."

Jim was a clerk in their cage at the bank and a student at NYU. Midge and Gerry hung on to every word he said, awed with his vocabulary—words like fetishes and Oedipus complex—like he was speaking in a foreign language. Midge added these words to the growing list of words she wrote down in her diary, along with Physiognomical Haircuts. She discovered that term over a barbershop in the subway, and she thought they were really good word to save.

Midge was sure she and Gerry were on their way to becoming Bohemians.

It was dark, usually, when they came back from walking the streets of Staten Island. Although there wasn't anything too exciting there, Midge just wanted to go somewhere without having to ask permission.

The automat was open late, so Midge and Gerry would stop in for their favorite supper of beans, Harvard beets, and apple pie.

At that time of night, most of the commuters had gone home; the few stragglers eating at the tables usually sat alone staring at their plates, and the only sounds were dishes of food dropping out of the slots.

Gerry would smear her lipstick and get tobacco all over her teeth. She kept picking bits of it out of her mouth, the whole time she drank her coffee. They didn't smoke much, actually they shared a pack of Pall Malls. Midge took the pack home one night and Gerry the next until the pack was empty.

Two months after Gerry came to work, Japan's sneak attack on Pearl Harbor plunged the country into World War II. Boys were drafted into the armed services, and during air raid drills, wardens patrolled the night streets reminding people to pull their blinds so as not to risk detection by enemy planes. The bank also hired Anna Mae.

Frilly, blonde, and bubbly, Anna Mae had a high, little-girl voice. On Monday mornings, she came to work so excited her breathing came in short little gasps.

"Oh, I had such a gorgeous weekend!" She told the entire cage of workers.

"Whatcha do?" Someone always egged her on.

"Well, me and my boyfriend, Bobby . . . he's in the Army you know . . . but he gets home every weekend, and we just have a swell time. We went dancing Saturday night and all we did was laugh and laugh and laugh."

Every single weekend, it seemed to Midge, Anna Mae and Bobby laughed for two days.

Midge and Gerry called her "Laughing Girl" and everyone in the cage laughed and laughed with her on Monday morning and thought she was amusing and cute. Jim analyzed her according to Freud and said. "Anna Mae was fixated in childhood."

Fred, the boss of the department, smiled at Anna Mae a lot. Gerry and Midge liked Fred, especially because he talked about his wife and kids. After a while, though, Midge and Gerry could tell that Laughing Girl was interested in Fred, too, only different. She giggled a lot and, whenever Fred was around, she did funny things with her eyes. It bothered Gerry more than it did Midge, who just wished she had a boyfriend.

Gerry would watch Anna Mae and squint her green eyes. Then she'd get so agitated she'd throw her head around till her hair swirled on her shoulders like a storm brewing. She'd clench her small teeth and ask Midge if she wanted to go for a smoke.

"Let's get outta here!" she'd say real loud, so the whole cage could hear. But in the lounge, she wouldn't talk except to ask, "We got any cigarettes left in that pack?"

Midge would scramble around in her bag for the pack of cigarettes while Gerry tapped her fingers on the arm of the couch and practically snatch the crumpled pack from Midge's hand. Then Gerry would puff away, one puff after another, until the cigarette was so small she couldn't put it out. She'd hold it between her forefinger and thumb and drop it into the cigarette receptacle.

Together they watched Fred get hooked on Laughing Girl so bad he could hardly act like a boss when she was around. After a while, he didn't talk about his wife anymore, and Laughing Girl didn't laugh and laugh with Bobby on weekends. Everyone in the cage knew what was happening and felt sorry for Fred. Gerry stopped talking to Laughing Girl.

On weekends, Gerry's church held dances for the neighborhood servicemen home on leave. Gerry went to meet guys. Midge wanted to go, too, but her mother said she couldn't go to Brooklyn for a whole weekend.

One Monday morning, Gerry came to work and looked as though she had slept in her clothes.

"What happened to you?" Midge asked. "You look terrible." Sometimes Gerry wore shoes that needed new heels, they were so run down, but Midge had never seen Gerry so messy.

"I'll tell you the whole lousy story later. Don't ask me any questions now, please." Gerry looked so sad, Midge wanted to say something nice, but she couldn't find the right words. So she just reminded Gerry she forgot to put on her mascara.

During one of their afternoon breaks, Gerry asked Midge, "Can you come home with me tonight?"

"I'll have to call home and ask my mother." Midge knew her mother would say no.

"I met a guy, Dave, Dave Kieslak." Gerry never stopped puffing. "I fell for him, I mean I really fell for the guy."

Sometimes, Midge felt so young. All she could ask was, "What happened?"

"We went to this dance last night. But Dave and I left early. We walked for hours just talking and holding hands. He said he wanted to see me again when he got another leave. He's in the Army. When he took me home, my sister and her husband were asleep, so we sat on the front porch."

Gerry stopped and just stared out, then she said. "I wasn't going to do anything in my sister's house, so we sat on the couch in the dark. Then he wanted to—you know?"

"What do you mean . . . you know?" Midge asked.

"You know, Midge, do it . . ." Gerry waved her cigarette around in the air, and cigarette ashes fell all over the floor.

"Oh, my God!"

"I told him I couldn't." Gerry defended herself. "But I said I loved him."

Midge was uncomfortable. "So then what did he say?"

"He said he couldn't love me. He was married."

"Married!" Midge jumped up from the lounge chair. "I can't believe it, and he wanted to...?"

Gerry put out her cigarette. "Yeh!"

"You can't see him anymore, Gerry." Midge stood near Gerry and looked down at her. "It would be a mortal sin, and you'll get pregnant."

"Yeh, I know, I know." Gerry brushed some ashes from her skirt and checked her wrist watch.

"We have to get back."

When she stood up, she didn't say anything. They walked to the elevator and pushed the down button.

"You think I would have guessed," Gerry said. They watched the brass arrow on the light panel over the elevator click off the floors. "How can you tell a guy is married? Anyhow, even if you know, he could still be on the prowl, like Fred."

"Fred wasn't on the prowl, Gerry," Midge said. "He's not like that. He's just friendly."

"Yeh, it was probably all Anna Mae's fault, flirting with him all the time."

"I dunno, Gerry. Sometimes I think Anna Mae's sorry she fell for Fred. She doesn't laugh anymore like she used to."

"She asked for it," Gerry said. "She shoulda known better, not to get mixed up with a married man."

"But maybe, at first she just liked him, like you did, Gerry. She didn't know that liking him was going to get her into trouble."

"Did I get into trouble?" Gerry glared at Midge. "Am I going to see Dave again?"

"Did you push our floor?"

Midge checked the panel. "We get off now. C'mon."

All the way back to the cage, they never said a word. Midge kept thinking about Fred and Anna Mae. Were they kidding themselves? Maybe they really just liked each other. Anyway, how do you fall in love, she asked herself. At the entrance to the cage, Gerry put her hand on Midge's arm.

"See if you can come home with me tonight. My sister and brother-in-law are going to Jersey to see his mother. I don't want to be alone."

Midge said she would call her mother—see what she could do. "But I'm going to have to tell her your sister is dying or something. 'Cause she only falls for sad stories, and that's the only way I'll get to come home with you."

Gerry rolled her eyes and shrugged her shoulders.

That night Midge and Gerry took the subway to Brooklyn.

The trains were hot and packed with commuters. Finally, they got off and climbed the cement steps to the street where the houses hugged each other for blocks. Gerry's sister lived in a brown-shingled house that sat on the edge of the sidewalk. When Gerry unlocked the back door, the air smelled stale in the small kitchen. Only one window looked out on the wall of the house next door.

"I wonder if my sister left anything to eat?"

Gerry opened the refrigerator and just stood staring into it.

"My sister is a rotten cook, and a terrible housekeeper. Good thing she has a really great husband."

"Do you look like your sister?" Midge asked.

"A little, only she's skinny and ten years older." Gerry searched in the cupboard. "Want some pork and beans? Some tomato soup? There's bread and butter . . . and tea."

"O.K. Sounds O.K."

They ate the soup hot, but ate the beans right out of the can, with bread and butter and lots of hot tea. They still had some cigarettes left, so they finished the pack before going to bed.

"We can sleep in my sister's bed. Usually I sleep here on the couch, 'cause they just don't have enough room."

Gerry gave Midge a nightgown. It must have been one of Gerry's, it was so wide and long. When they turned out the light, Gerry wanted to talk.

"I really thought I'd found someone special." Gerry lay on her back, her arms at her side.

"I'm sorry," Midge said, "I really am. I'm sorry you had to meet such a jerk."

"He said it didn't matter if he was married. He liked me."

But Gerry was talking to herself. "I tried to talk myself into seeing him again, but I couldn't."

"Midge," Gerry turned to her, "Why did Laughing Girl haffta stop laughing?"

Midge knew Gerry was crying, so she put her arm around her friend and said, "Ssssh, go to sleep."

They lay there quiet, and after a while Gerry's breathing came low and steady. But Midge was wide awake thinking about Ruth and Jane and Irish track stars, and trying to sort out Laughing Girl, all frilly and looking sad, with her little girl voice. And Gerry, so lonely and angry, even though she had a swell sister who Midge never met, but who had to be real nice to let Gerry sleep on the couch.

And Mama. She had tried so hard to get Midge to be a telephone operator in New Jersey. It seemed such a long time ago that she heard her mother say, "But Midgie, listen to your mother. Telephone operators get a lot of benefits. Silk stockings, Midgie. You can't get them with the war going on."

That night Midge lay awake a long time thinking about silk stockings.

# The Parrot

On early summer evenings after the sun disappeared behind the houses, the Italians sat on Tony's front stoop drinking wine and smoking roll-your-own cigarettes, waiting for the fireflies, listening to the quiet and missing the sound of kids playing ball in the once-open field, now overgrown with small, identical houses.

Out of a habit that began during the war years when cigarettes were scarce, the men rolled their own with loose tobacco and papers. Ten years later, the habit was hard to give up. The Italians could no more let it go than they could stop making their own wine and bootleg whiskey. They felt that way about the neighborhood, too—letting it go, that is. There were some changes since the war ended. A few more cars, a little more money in their pockets, families grown up. And strangers moving into what they always considered their private piece of town put frowns on their faces.

Tony took a drag on his cigarette.

"Hey, Fausto, look who's coming across the street."

"He's coming over here." Fausto leaned back against the cement step. "Why the hell is he coming over here now? He never crossed this street since 1935, the last time he made such a stink when the kids hit a ball in his garden."

The street was a narrow road where, before the war, few cars traveled, and grass grew between the small stones up through the sifted, soft dirt the kids pretended was flour when they played "store." The road was also considered a buffer between the kids in the neighborhood and Gus, the German "grouch." Gus lived in the white bungalow on the corner along with his mother, before she passed away, and a noisy parrot. As far as the neighborhood parents were concerned, if they ever sat down and gave it some thought, the road was an ocean between the Italians and the German, and that's the way they liked it.

The Italians sat motionless. Their eyes followed the short, stocky man dressed in brown work pants and checkered shirt. He was balancing a parrot on his shoulder and pushing a red wheelbarrow filled with vegetables across the dirt road in their direction.

The grin across his face looked like it was pasted on.

"Good evening," he called out. As if he'd been visiting the Italians every night for the past twenty years, without a misstep in his plans, he settled the wheelbarrow down carefully on the sidewalk and leaned against the stone wall that ran in front of the house.

"Nice evening," he continued. "Nice."

Fausto waited for Tony to say something first. He wasn't sure how to act; he'd let Tony make the first move. Tony was hanging on tight to his glass of wine and when he finally found his voice, he tried to disguise what he was feeling, not to sound as though Gus weren't welcome.

"How are you? Here, sit down." Tony moved over on the step to make room, "Have a glass of wine."

"No, no, I don't drink. No offense," Gus said matter-of-fact like. "Just lemonade." For a moment, Gus turned away and looked toward the bungalow across the street and lapsed into a reverie. "I miss my mother's lemonade and cookies on these warm days."

The Italians exchanged that "poor bastard" look. But they weren't sure they were ready to cross out the past, to let it all go with the Depression and the war.

In all the years they'd lived within shouting distance of each other, few words passed between Gus and the Italians. Mostly "Good morning," and "Good evening." Sometimes, "Nice day" might follow whenever the Italians met Gus's mother, a little woman and a devout Lutheran who they referred to as "that poor old lady" sweeping the sidewalk in front of her bungalow. Anyone who could live with "the Black Hun"—the Italians reserved that name for Gus's father—deserved to be pitied.

On the other hand, the Germans didn't understand the Italians either—why they laughed so much and so loud, why they let their kids run loose in the neighborhood, hit balls into the German's crafted gardens and then asked for the balls to be returned. So the Italians and the Germans had long decided by their silence, the neighborhood was better off if each knew his boundary. Ever since Gus and the Italians were young men, they honored their differences.

Still, the Italians figured Gus was lonely with both his parents gone and no siblings to keep him company. He had no one left except the parrot. A cousin, Althea, a stern, spinster who lived up the road, was his only living relative, and she rarely visited Gus except to reprimand him about something.

"Well, take a load off your feet. Sit down. But watch that parrot. I don't want him biting me." Tony looked at the parrot and scowled.

"She don't bite. She gives kisses. She's a good girl. Here, Tony," Gus moved closer to Tony and took the parrot off his shoulder. "Here, let her give you a kiss. She likes you."

Tony threw back his head and put out his hand. "If that bird kisses me, I'll kick his ass."

"Ah! don't say that, Tony. Hilda will feel bad."

Gus put Hilda back on his shoulder, assuring her, "Tony won't hurt you."

"Father didn't like children coming into the yard or the house," Gus turned to the Italians, as though he needed to explain. "So, Mother thought Hilda would be nice for me. She was very kind, you know."

The Italians said nothing. What could they say. Gus was an old man, and he never had anybody.

"So, Gus, what's new?" Tony tried to lighten things up. Make them all feel more comfortable.

"Well, I brought over some vegetables from the garden. It's the last garden I'll have. I just sold part of my land, the part with the garden and the garage. The house is enough for me."

"You sold the property?" Tony asked. "To who? When? Jesus. We didn't know a thing about it."

"I signed the papers just a few days ago. When the doctor told me to take it easy, my heart was no good anymore, that's when I decided to sell."

"Yeh," Fausto said, "I thought I saw some funny people around the place, but I didn't think you sold the property. It's right across from me. What kind of house they gonna put up? Not some big Barrakka, I hope."

"I don't know, Fausto. It's not my property anymore. But I think the real estate man said they're Porter Ricans. You know, they're like the Japs who live at the end of the road. Only I think the Japs are quiet. What are you going to do? You have to sell to whoever has the money. It's not the way it used to be."

"Nothing ain't the same," Tony said. Gus had turned the evening around, and exposed things the Italians were not ready to face.

"But, Gus," Tony quickly changed the subject. "I'm sorry to hear about your heart. You gotta be careful. But now maybe you could have some fun. That won't hurt you."

"Well, actually, I was thinking of joining a German-American club over in the city," Gus said. "Maybe go on some trips, you know, meet some people who I can talk German with, like you gentlemen, with your Italian friends, you know. . . ."

"That's a good idea, Gus. Bravo for you. Is your cousin up the road still butting in your business?"

Gus smiled. "We won't tell her what we're doing."

"Well," Tony took a drag on his cigarette, "she'll never get it out of us. Hell, she don't even look at us when we meet her."

And that's how it began.

Gus joined a German-American club and every once in a while, he walked over and briefed the Italians on what was happening.

"Any good-looking ladies?" they asked, winking at each other.

Gus blushed. "Just friendly ladies. I like it that way."

The summer days drifted into Autumn, and Gus and Hilda

came regularly to visit with Tony and Fausto. None of them were big talkers, a single sentence every now and then, never about anything very important, mostly they talked about the weather, how the neighborhood was changing, and now and again they fell into a nostalgic place and that always led to heavy silence and eventually someone said, "Guess, it's time to go in."

When the weather turned cold, Tony and Fausto often met in Tony's basement. Gus was real glad when they invited him to join them, and so through the winter months the three men sat around the asbestos-covered furnace and kept each other company.

Once, Tony's wife asked him. "So what do you men do down there?"

"Talk," Tony said. "Just talk."

Rose wanted to know exactly what they talked about and what about that bird?

"About what? We talk. You, know, just like when you get together with the ladies. You talk. Right?" Tony didn't like getting into these conversations with Rose when she picked at him, pick, pick, piece by piece, just like when she picked at the left-over chicken after Sunday dinner.

"Well," she said, "you must talk about something. I can't imagine you men just sitting down there looking at the furnace all night. What does the old German have to say? Doesn't he tell you anything about the club he belongs to? Doesn't he?" And she gave Tony this dirty look. "Doesn't he talk about any woman?"

"Gus ain't interested in any woman. He's got Hilda."

"Well, if you ask me, that's kinda strange, that's all I gotta say about that. And one thing I want to remind you, I don't ever want to see that bird dirtying up my basement. You make sure of that, or out goes Gus and the bird."

Tony just shook his head. When he thought about the parrot these days, inside him somewhere he was glad Gus had her. It wasn't something he would talk about, especially not to Rose.

"You have nothing to worry about," Tony told his wife. "Gus and Hilda have nobody, so we all get together and keep each other company. We're neighbors, that's all."

The winter nights slipped by, and the wood stacks outside the basement door grew smaller. The men began to talk about spring.

"I think," Gus told the men one night, "the club is planning some good trips this spring and summer."

Tony remembered his trip across the Atlantic Ocean when, as a young man, he came to America, but he never thought of it as a "good trip," something to get excited about. It was something he wanted to forget; the long days of waves tossing the ship as though it were a toy, vomiting everything he ate, and the closeness of people, all kinds of people, looking forward to a new country but not knowing what to expect. He asked no questions when Gus talked about the trips the club would make. He did not want to remember.

Spring came early and by May, the men were sitting out on the stoop evenings, drinking wine and smoking cigarettes.

One evening, the Italians were just about ready to call it a day as the spring evening cooled when they saw Gus running across the street, waving something in his hand above his head.

"Tony! Fausto! I'm going to Disneyland."

Suddenly the words trailed off as though he were gasping for breath. He tried to call out again, but his voice sounded like it was catching on something.

"Hilda, Tony...Hilda..."

Before the Italians could get to him, Gus collapsed on the street like a pile of old clothes, still clutching the paper in his hand.

"Jesus," Tony yelled. "Gus, are you all right?"

Tony knelt down and put his hand on Gus's neck, then he put his ear to Gus's mouth. He looked up at Fausto, who looked down at them with his mouth open.

"Fausto, I think Gus is dead!"

"Oh! Sacramento!"

Fausto started to walk away in confusion. Then he turned back to Tony. "What should we do? Should I call the police?"

Tony shook his head. "No, call Mr. Mahoney, the undertaker. He'll know what to do. And Fausto, somebody has to tell the old crab up the road."

"Not me," Fausto said, shaking his head back and forth. "Not me. You tell her."

"Okay. But first things first."

Fausto left to call Mr. Mahoney, and Tony sat down alongside Gus and took the paper from his hand. It was a plane ticket to Disneyland. All paid for, ready for Gus to have some fun, and now the poor bastard was dead.

When Fausto returned, Tony held it out to his friend. "It's a plane reservation,"

Fausto's eyes widened, and he took the paper. "Jesus, what are you gonna do with it, Tony? You gonna go to Disneyland?"

"Hell, no," Tony's face tightened. "We ain't gonna use it, and we ain't gonna let the old lady up the street have it either. We're gonna let Gus take it with him."

Fausto shook his head back and forth like there was something rattling around in it he didn't understand. "What the hell are you talking about? You don't make any sense."

Tony stood up. "We're gonna put the ticket in the casket with Gus, that's what I'm saying. We're not gonna let that old fool up the road get the money back. Gus was gonna go on that plane and have some fun, and he's gonna have that ticket with him wherever he's going next."

Fausto put his hands in his pants pockets and rocked forward and backward.

"I'm not saying a word to Angela. Right?"

"We're not telling your wife. We're not telling my wife. We're not telling anybody."

After Mr. Mahoney arrived with a policeman and they took Gus away, Tony and Fausto let themselves into Gus's house to find Hilda. She was balancing on the homemade perch Gus had made for her in the living room.

"We gotta figure out what to do with her." Tony took her down from the perch and put food and water in her trays. After she had eaten, they put her back on the perch, locked up and left.

Tony called Mr. Mahoney the next day and inquired what was going to happen to Gus. He would be laid out on the following day and buried after that, Mr. Mahoney assured Tony. Gus's cousin would be in charge of his affairs and if Tony had any questions, he should get in touch with Althea.

"That's it, Fausto, we have to put the plane reservation in the casket with Gus tomorrow. So this is what we are going to do. We are going to take Hilda with us..."

"To the funeral home? They'll kick us out."

"You'll see, Fausto, just follow me."

The next afternoon, Tony and Fausto were about to enter the funeral parlor with Hilda sitting on Tony's shoulder when Mr. Mahoney stopped them.

"Just a moment. You can't bring a parrot into the funeral parlor!" he said.

"She's Gus's friend, Mr. Mahoney. She's been with Gus since he was a kid. She just wants to say goodbye."

Mr. Mahoney shook his head. "She's not just a friend, she's a parrot, an animal, a bird. And animals are not permitted in the funeral parlor. I'm sorry, I really am." Tony was just about to object again, but Mr. Mahoney interrupted. "What if she got loose? Can you imagine a parrot flying around in one of the rooms where a loved one is resting?"

Tony frowned. "She's ninety years old. She can't fly anymore. If you were ninety years old, could you fly?"

Mr. Mahoney arched his eyebrows, but before he could answer, Tony continued.

"We won't be long. Just a few minutes and anyway I betcha there's nobody in there visiting Gus. I betcha he's all alone. So why can't his best friend just say goodbye?"

Mahoney's Funeral Parlor had preserved and sent many of Tony's and Fausto's family on their final journey, so Mr. Mahoney was eager to oblige, but at the same time, he did not want to encourage unconventional behavior.

"I'm sorry, but no live animals are allowed in the mortuary. I'm sorry." His voice was low and soft, but the Italians knew he meant business.

"Well, then, Mr. Mahoney, you hold her for us till we say goodbye to Gus." Tony handed Hilda to Mr. Mahoney, who reached out for the parrot before Tony could let her fall to the floor.

"But, Tony, just a moment...I can't...Tony, this is ridiculous."

But the Italians were already on their way to the room where

Gus was laid out. The only guests in the small room were two men, probably from the Lutheran church, and Gus's cousin, Althea.

"She's here, Fausto. Keep close to me when we get to the coffin, so when I put the airline ticket in his jacket pocket, that nosey cousin won't see what I'm doing. Bow your head and pray, you know, look like you're saying the rosary or something."

The two men walked toward the coffin slowly with their heads bowed. When Althea looked up and saw them, she pursed her lips in disapproval, pursed them so hard, they looked like a thin line drawn across her face.

"Just a moment," she said. "You know I'm Gus's only relative and I will be cleaning up the house and putting it on the market, so you won't be going in and out like it was 'open house.' I suppose you have been looking after that bird." She pursed her lips again.

Tony was taken by surprise. Not that he didn't expect something like this, but Gus wasn't even cold in his grave yet.

"Whadda ya gonna to do with that parrot?" Tony asked,

"Well," Althea showed no sympathy. "I thought I would call the SPCA. They would take care of him."

"Jesus," Tony said. "They could give Hilda to some people who wouldn't understand her, or some kid who might pull out her feathers. You can't do that."

"Well, if you have a better idea, you can take responsibility for the bird."

"I will," Tony said. "Fausto and I will do something. Leave Hilda to us." The Italians moved closer to the casket and each other until they looked as though they were stitched together. Tony removed the envelope with the airline ticket from his vest pocket.

"Pray, Fausto," he whispered, and as he leaned over the body, he slid the envelope inside Gus's jacket.

On their way out, they stopped in front of Althea, and Tony patted her on the shoulder. "Now, don't you worry about Hilda. Fausto and me are going to take good care of her, and by tomorrow we'll know exactly what to do with her, so you won't have to worry about one more thing. OK? We're just good neighbors." Althea looked up at him suspiciously, but never said a word.

Mr. Mahoney was waiting for them and, surprisingly, he seemed to be enjoying Hilda.

That night Tony and Fausto entered the quiet house. It smelled of being closed up, leftover food, and Hilda's bedding. Even the smell of aging furniture crowded the house.

"Boy, this place needs to be aired out," Fausto said. "If Angela ever came in here, Sacramento! I have to cook my baccalà in the cellar with the windows open, so the stink don't get upstairs."

Tony wasn't listening. "What are we gonna do with Hilda? Tomorrow is the funeral. We got to think fast, so forget the stink, think about Hilda."

"She should be going with Gus," Fausto said. "But how we gonna put her in the casket? Even if we could, what if she started singing 'Polly wants a cracker'? Mr. Mahoney's gonna know that ain't Gus."

Fausto laughed. "Poor Mr. Mahoney, he might give up the undertaker job." Tony sat in one of the overstuffed chairs studying Hilda on her perch while Hilda studied Tony.

"Stop with the jokes, Fausto. Think. We have to come up with something."

"Well, I guess it would be easy if Hilda was dead," Fausto offered.

"Dead?" Tony repeated. "If Hilda was dead."

Tony's face suddenly broke out in a smile, almost a laugh. "That's it. If she's dead!"

"What the hell are you talking about, Tony?"

"Just this." Tony went over and pointed to the clothes basket that sat under the perch heaped to the top with shredded pieces of newspaper.

"Sometimes, Gus said Hilda falls off the perch, so he filled the basket with paper nice and soft, so she won't hurt herself. But if we take away the nice bed tonight and Hilda falls off the perch, you know, 'cause she's so old, well…We'll stop around in the morning before the funeral and then we'll see…"

Fausto looked at Tony and his face squinted like a kid learning his alphabet. "You mean, we should kill her?"

"We're not gonna kill her. If she falls off her perch, it'll be fate.

Dontcha see, it means her time came, just like all of us. If it was meant to be, we have no control. I think somebody wrote all about that, a long time ago, maybe in the Bible. Everything is in the Bible. See?"

Fausto scratched his head. He did see, but wasn't sure they were going to get off the hook so easy. "Then what? What do we do with the bird? Throw her in the garbage?"

"No, no, no. Then we put her in the casket with Gus. That's where she belongs. With Gus. Mary won't let me take her home. She says no birds in the house. She's not cleaning up bird shit. So this way, nobody has to worry about Hilda anymore, and Hilda is happy going to wherever Gus is going."

Fausto wasn't sure he was on board completely. Killing off the bird wasn't what he would have thought of at first, but then, what the hell, he wasn't going to take Hilda, so what Tony suggested was probably the best way out.

"Okay. So should we take out all the shredded paper?"

"Yeh. Just empty it."

"You know, Tony, I just got to thinkin'. You think Mr. Mahoney is going to let us put Hilda in the casket with Gus? After the way he acted today, it don't seem to me that he's going to let us put Hilda in the casket, just like that."

Tony sat in one of the chairs and for a few minutes said nothing. Fausto waited. He knew soon or later, Tony would have something to say. Tony just liked to take his time when he was thinking, like waiting for the wine they made every Fall, it took time to get better.

"Yeh, I think you're right," he said finally. "This is what we're gonna have to do. We'll wait till Mr. Mahoney tells everybody to leave. Then I'll ask him, please, could I have just a few minutes alone with Gus before he closes the casket. I'll say I want to say some things to Gus that are personal, you know, some stuff I don't want anybody to hear before Gus is gone. I'll make it sound real good. But it means, I'll tell him, I have to be alone with Gus. Then I'll put Hilda in the casket and I'll close it. I'm just hoping when he comes back he'll think one of the other guys who work for him closed it, and that will be that."

Fausto nodded his head up and down like he was a puppet.

"Sounds good, if it all goes the way you say. If not, then..."

"We'll worry about that then," Tony said.

He got up and went over to Hilda, who was standing on her perch watching them. The men stood there a long time looking at the parrot before Tony said, "Don't look sad, Hilda." He put his cheek next to Hilda's beak. "Here, gimme a kiss. You can gimme a kiss, and I won't kick your ass. Okay."

Tony felt a slight peck. Son of a bitch, he thought. He just let a parrot kiss him.

"Ciao, Hilda. Be a good girl."

The next morning, the Italians went back to Gus's house before they left for the funeral. "You go first, Tony." Fausto stood aside at the door and let Tony step into the living room.

"She's in the basket, Fausto." The two men looked down at the parrot lying sideways in the basket very still, and very stiff.

"I think she's dead, Fausto."

"Jesu Christo! We shoulda known. I feel bad. Now what are we going to do?"

"Exactly what we talked about last night. We got no time to stop and cry over things. See if you can find a paper bag in the kitchen, so we can put Hilda in it."

Fausto came back with a bag and they carefully put the parrot in it.

Tony looked into the bag a few minutes and then he said, "Rose is going to be nosey and want to know what I have in the bag. I guess I'm gonna have to tell her. She's gonna be mad. I only hope she doesn't get stupid and I have to leave Hilda home."

"Give her to me then, Tony. Angela doesn't ask questions like Rose. Then I'll give her back to you before you talk to Mr. Mahoney."

"Good," Tony said. "That's good. OK, let's go."

There were only a handful of people in Gus's room, Althea and a few Lutherans from the church. Since Tony and Fausto and their wives weren't going to the graveyard, the women wanted to leave early. Tony had to convince his wife and Angela to stay.

"Look, we ain't gonna see Gus again. A little more time isn't gonna hurt you. I want to stay till it's time to go."

Rose and Angela both stood up from the wooden seats. "Stay if you want to. We're going. We'll probably shop on the way home, so we'll see you later." The two women made one last trip to the casket, knelt down and said a prayer, made the sign of the cross, offered their condolences to Althea, and left.

The Italians sat silently playing with their hats to pass the time. Fausto dropped his once and Tony frowned.

Then Mr. Mahoney, came into the room, and in a solemn voice he had been practicing for years, he announced to the mourners that it was time to leave, they would be closing the casket. Althea and the others paid their last visit and left. Mr. Mahoney, when he noticed that the Italians hadn't moved, looked at Tony and Fausto questioningly.

"Time to leave, gentlemen."

Fausto toyed with his hat, but Tony spoke up. "Fausto is leaving, but I have a big favor to ask you. You see, I want to say a few things to Gus, secret things I don't want nobody to hear, and this is the last time I'll have a chance, so I thought I could have just a few extra minutes, alone with Gus."

Mr. Mahoney did not look happy. "You could have said them before this."

"How could I? There was always somebody here. What I want to say is very personal. Very personal. Just between me and Gus. If he goes before I have a chance to tell him, I'll have it on my conscience for the rest of my life. A few minutes. That's all. My family has been a good customer, Mr. Mahoney, and we'll go on being good customers, so a little favor won't hurt."

Mr. Mahoney didn't like ruffling feathers. "Very well, I guess a few extra minutes won't hurt. You're leaving, Fausto, is that right?"

Fausto nodded.

As Mr. Mahoney walked away, Fausto slipped the bag to Tony and then left. Tony approached the casket and looked around before he took Hilda out of the bag. Carefully, he patted down some feathers that were out of place. Then he folded the parrot and placed her on Gus's shoulder. "That's good. Nice. Just the way it should be. Everybody has a right to something in this life, otherwise why the hell are we here. You had a right, too, Gus, to go Disneyland and to have Hilda buried with you."

Tony gave Gus a pat on the hand.

"Ciao, Gus, maybe we'll meet again, if not . . . hey," and then he pulled down the lid. It snapped closed. "It's right this way."

He quickly made the sign of the cross, just in case, and breathed a sigh of relief. Now if Mr. Mahoney doesn't question the closed casket.

As he was about to leave, Mr. Mahoney came back in. He looked at the coffin, puzzled, as though he were trying to remember if he had shut the lid. But Tony thought fast, took out his handkerchief and starting wiping at his eyes.

"We were good friends, Mr. Mahoney, lived near each other for over 50 years. You know what that means, Mr. Mahoney?"

He was thinking only of distracting the funeral director, but he realized that it wasn't just Gus who died. The empty spot Gus left in the neighborhood was the end of an era, a time that would never come again.

The neighborhood was changing. Strangers were moving in. Tony knew he had to get used to them even though they weren't like the Germans, the Irish, or the Italians, his neighbors up and down the street.

He wasn't sure if he would ever get used to the new ways.

Mr. Mahoney patted Tony on the shoulder. "I'm very sorry. I had no idea you and Mr. Brown were such good friends." Then he instructed his workers to bring the casket to the car standing outside.

Fausto was waiting at the foot of the stairs, turning his hat over and over in his hand. When he saw Tony, he hesitated.

"Is everything all right?" he asked.

Tony kept right on walking. "Everything is good, Fausto. Just the way the end should be."

# Promises, Promises, Promises

March, 1984

I just realized we are three weeks into the Lenten season and I still haven't drawn up my sacrifice list of "wills and won'ts."

In my childhood, those promises were draped in purple and scrupulously honored from Ash Wednesday to Easter Sunday. The number of years since my last list could almost fill one end of an hourglass, but I still remember the zeal we attached to the pre-Easter season.

So, I peered through time and recreated a list that I might have made in those sweet lost days of innocence and faithfulness.

My List for Lent

1. I promise to put all the pennies Mama gives me Sunday morning into the Church collection basket and not spend it on candy.

2. I promise not to make my brother Junior, who has infantile paralysis and wears a brace on his leg, go upstairs ahead of me in the dark to turn on the light after we listen to "The Witches Tale" on the radio.

3. I promise not to keep Mama waiting when she wants me to do dishes and I'm reading a book in the bathroom.

4. I promise not to read the writing on the walls of the underpass

near the high school, even if I did find out what Helen Watson did on Saturday night back in the cemetery.

5. I promise to pay attention in class, especially arithmetic. But I wish Sister wouldn't draw a picture of a pie on the blackboard when she teaches fractions. It makes me hungry.

6. I promise not to laugh at Nancy Coucci if a bee stings her tongue again when she's eating a jelly sandwich.

7. I promise not to go to any of the movies on the Condemned List. Except I don't understand why they put "Ah! Wilderness" on it.

8. I promise not to laugh at Sister when she uses holy water to bless a key stuck in the cloakroom door.

9. I promise to collect a lot of tinfoil from empty cigarette packs so Sister can send it to the pagans in China.

10.  I promise not to make Mama run around the dining room table to catch me when I'm bad. She's old, and maybe she could have a heart attack.

11. I promise not to wipe off Grandma's kisses even when they're sloppy.

12. I promise to be very holy on Good Friday. I won't talk all day, and I'll stay in church, and I'll be very sad. But after I get home, I better keep out of Mama's way, 'cause Mama gets nervous when I get too holy.

13. I promise not to ring crabby old Althea's doorbell and run and hide during Lent.

14. When we sing the "Litany of the Saints" on Easter Saturday morning, I promise not to sing "Lead us out on a stormy day" instead of "Liberamus Domine," even if the other kids do, 'cause Sister Anthony gets mad and yells, "All right, you guys, cut it out," and I shouldn't make her yell just before Jesus rises from the dead.

15. I promise not to swipe cookies out of Mr. Kearney's store, even if he does know but makes believe he doesn't see us.

16. When we play movie stars, I promise not to pretend to be Mae West, 'cause she's on the Condemned List. I sure like the way she walks, though.

17. I promise not to make up any gossip so Mama will pay attention when I talk to her. When I told Mama that Rose McGill

had to leave school 'cause she was going to have a baby by some sailor she met when the fleet came in, Mama didn't stop talking about it for days. I won't make up a story like that again.

18. I promise not to look at pictures of people without their clothes on in the National Geographic.

19. I promise not to laugh at Sister Matrona when she uses the pitch pipe and sings the first note. And even if her voice sounds like she's gargling during music, she looks like she's going to cry when the class snickers, and I feel real bad. Maybe, God, you could give her laryngitis.

20. I promise not to speak about that bad, bad word again, ever since me and my cousins were talking about it in the empty coal bin down in the cellar. My mother and my aunt overheard us and made us come up and explain what we knew about "it," which was nothing. But it had to be important, because somebody printed it in letters three feet high on the wall of the underpass.

21. I promise to be so good during Lent that I'll probably go right to heaven if I get hit by a trolley car before I can get to Confession. If I don't die before Easter Sunday, I hope the sun shines so I can wear my white shoes to 9 o'clock Mass. I hope Mama remembers to buy some jellybeans to put around the cut-glass bowl of colored eggs on the dining room table. Mama will make sweet bread and home-made noodles. And maybe she'll get to change her housedress by the afternoon, so she can enjoy the relatives who visit while we kids go to the movies.

22. I promise not to sneak into the movies on Saturday afternoon. You're gonna have to find me some money, God, to pay to get in, 'cause I already promised not to keep the collection pennies.

23. I promise, and it's going to be hard, not to get mad at Father Murphy when he tells us on St. Patrick's day that the best mothers in the world are Irish, and my mother is Italian.

These promises usually came to Easter Sunday in shreds, just a few bearing any resemblance to their original shining intent. But I knew that Easter Sunday would still dawn as bright as a yellow jellybean, and next year I would try again. That is, of course, if I didn't get hit by a trolley car that summer.

# Forever Rebecca

On the spring day my husband announced we were moving to Vermont, I resisted.

"Uh-uh!" I said, "Not unless I can have a rooster."

Why did I say that? Were spring breezes softening my brain?

Or was I remembering another rooster-in-residence from years past, an industrious bird who performed his daily ritual at dawn alongside the old weather vane atop the hen house in my aunt's backyard. I was certain that rooster crowed every morning just for me.

Perhaps that was it.

Somewhere, I suspect, in that vast labyrinth of childhood memories, I sheltered an image of myself as Rebecca of Sunnybrook Farm, gathering eggs in a little basket as chickens clucked gently in the kitchen dooryard.

"O.K.," Ted conceded. "And how about some hens to keep him company, Midge?"

We had a deal, and the image of Rebecca faded back into memory as more practical and urgent tasks such as buying a house absorbed my attention.

We took hurried trips to Vermont to select a location. With the competitive assistance of no fewer than four realtors and two intense weeks of "…and this is the kitchen," "…the living room needs some work," and "…it's still cheaper than real estate in New

Jersey," we settled on an old farmhouse, a handy man's special with a lot of promise.

The house sat back from a dirt road on six acres of velvet pasture cut through by a brook that ran cold and clear next to a huge red barn with its very own hen house.

In early August, we packed our belongs into a moving van, shed tears with our married children, swore to keep in touch with friends, and waved farewell to the Garden State.

At last, Rebecca dear, I was going to be countrified.

Shortly after settling into the rhythm of Vermont country living, Ted and I bought our first batch of chickens. An old timer in the valley was culling out his flock, and he let us have fifteen assorted hens, Rhode Island reds and Plymouth Rocks, for a song. A dashing rooster, enormously plump, his comb peaked in symmetrical spikes over sharp, narrow eyes kept the hens in line.

We called him Sylvester. He strutted around the barnyard, displaying bright red feathers with a sweeping iridescent black tail, like a sheik supervising his harem. I could hardly wait for next morning to hear his noble "Cock-a-doodle-do."

Sylvester didn't disappoint me. His no-nonsense call commanded, "Get up! Get up!"

Obediently, I fetched my antique egg basket and strode out to the hen house. Pushing open the heavy wooden door, I stepped inside the newly white-washed room. It resonated with a low chicken sound like so much grumbling. Some of the hens were poised like tightrope performers on their roosts while a few squatted on their nests producing their quota of eggs. Others wandered about clucking softly under their breath, "This is my day off."

Sylvester approached me with slow, deliberate steps. I swung my basket gaily at my side and greeted the hens.

"Good morning, girls."

Sylvester came closer.

"Nice rooster," I purred, but before I had a chance to inspect any of the nests for eggs, Sylvester puffed up his feathers and charged. I waved the empty egg basket at him, but he kept coming. I retreated quickly, shrieking "Down, boy, down!," and backed out the door. I tried to be rational about his behavior. Sylvester felt threatened, no doubt. He probably required more time to adjust to his new surroundings.

But the next day, he attacked again, and I was forced to play a new game. I grabbed an empty grain bag and waved it at him. "Toro!" I shouted, planting my feet firmly on the cement floor. Sylvester didn't understand my Spanish challenge, and his sharp peak pecked at the bag with the persistence of a jackhammer.

Rebecca was no match for this warrior rooster. Again, I retreated in defeat.

On the third day, I prepared for my outing to the henhouse carrying a large cardboard shield and a straw broom. It was tricky fending off Sylvester, but I soon discovered that vigorous broomwork kept him off balance, mostly off his feet . . . actually, he flew a lot.

Whatever eggs I could find, I quickly stuffed into my pockets. So much for the tidy little basket.

After that, time and time again I made overtures to Sylvester. I was chatty. I was aloof. I was a friend. I was Goliath.

Nothing worked.

Sylvester's behavior eloquently informed me that I was, and ever would be, an intruder in his realm.

We had decided our chickens would roam free on the range, as they say in the country. It was a bucolic scene, chickens in the dooryard executing their quaint choreography, two steps forward, one step back, scratching the ground and pecking at whatever they peck at.

Sylvester kept himself busy alternating between servicing the hens and chasing me around the yard. One fall morning, I was making an attempt to be punctual for an appointment to have snow tires put on the car and keep a luncheon date with a friend. When I approached the driver's side of the car, Sylvester was standing guard. I slowed down, giving him time to withdraw. I came to a halt when I realized that Sylvester had no intention of moving on.

"Shoo," I said. His eyes seemed to narrow as he planned his attack.

"Help" I cried as we went round and round the car, Sylvester at my heels, flapping his wings and extending his spurs. He would have followed me into the kitchen, but I slammed the screen door on his beak.

"That's it!" I screamed. "It's either me or that nasty rooster. One of us has got to go."

Ted was having a leisurely lunch, and he looked up surprised. "What do you want me to do?" he asked.

I don't know how Rebecca of Sunnybrook Farm would have dealt with Sylvester's antics, but at that moment, I concluded, the only good rooster was a dead rooster.

"Off with his head," I said, forgetting that Ted took everything I said literally.

So much for Sylvester.

Anyway, Rebecca honey, wouldn't a few, fleecy sheep look sweet, bleating playfully on the velvet pastures?

# Everybody is Dying Down Here

"Hello . . ."

"Hello, Midgie?"

"Yes. Is that you, Mama?"

"Yeh. How are you?"

"Oh, super, Mama. How are you?"

"LOUSY!"

"Oh, come on now, Mama. You sound terrific. Your voice is improving. It's so much stronger. What did the doctor say?"

"You think I sound better?"

"Two hundred per cent. You can hardly tell you had any trouble at all."

"Well, I went to the doctor the other day, you know. And he says, let's face it, I got hardening of the arteries in the head."

"What does that mean, Mama?"

"Well, he says that's why I get those funny feelings in my head. That's why I got a stroke. Whew! I'm tired. I just got back from your sister's."

"How is she?"

"She's a crab. I stayed a while, then when I got the fidgets, I came home."

"That sounds like a sensible thing to do. No use hanging around driving everybody crazy."

"Guess who dropped dead, Midgie."

"Who?"

"Old Man Brown."

"No!"

"Yeh! Monday, I saw him pushing the wheelbarrow in the backyard full of those rotten cabbages he gets from the vegetable store for compost. Tuesday, he dropped dead. And Friday, they burned him."

"Seems like just yesterday we kids were singing, 'Old Man Brown had a pimple on his belly, his mother cut it off and used it for jelly,' and he'd chase us all over the field where the development went in. Now he's dead."

"Everbody is dyin' down here, Midgie. Right and left. I'm goin' to a wake tomorrow. Remember Mimi Sireno?"

"Isn't she the one who moved over from the Bronx right after the war, and then made such a fuss because we didn't have any sidewalks?"

"That's the snot nose. Well, it wasn't her, it was her mother. I'm telling you, Midgie, I don't feel so good."

"Do you have any help down there, Mama? Does Joe come over and give you a hand?"

"You have a lousy brother."

"Now, Mama, he's not that bad."

"He's no good. I called him, and I says, 'Joe, I'll buy the paint for the hall upstairs and my bedroom. Will you paint them for me?'"

"Well....."

"'I have to check with the doctor,' he says."

"What doctor?"

"His wife, who do you think?"

"Oh!"

"So then he calls and says he can't. Get Manfred to do it."

"Well, that's too bad about him, Mama. Just some painting wouldn't kill him."

"I let that go. Manfred painted for me, and he did a swell job. So then I says, okay, now I'll see if that Joe will help me move the furniture around."

"Which furniture?"

"I want to move all the bedrooms around."

"So, what did he have to say this time?"

"Well, he says he has to check with the doctor again."

"What's the matter with him, anyway? Can't he do anything without his wife's permission?"

"I'm gonna wait now and see. And I swear on my mother's grave, if he doesn't come and help me, I'm cutting him out of my will."

"Mama, you're funny."

"You think I'm fooling, huh? I mean it. One dollar, I'll leave him."

"You can leave his share to me."

"You think I'm kidding. I'm not."

"Not to change the subject, Mama, but Ted and I are thinking of moving again."

"Again! Where? Why?"

"As a matter of fact, we were thinking of moving back down there."

"Don't do it! You're crazy. Everybody is dying down here."

"Oh, Mama. Everybody is dying all over the place. People are dying up here, too."

"Yeh, but not like down here. Five people died on the block this past year."

"That doesn't mean you have a priority or something. Anyway, where did you get five from?"

"First of all, it was Roger. Remember, the old guy on a pension who lived with the Beyers. Then the Frenchman, Mr. LeBlanc, or whatever his name was. He fell, poor devil, in front of the subway train..."

"Oh, God, Mama. That must have been awful. Wasn't his wife that Greek woman you couldn't understand?"

"Yeh! She drank."

"Did she take it hard?"

"Who knows? She's drunk all the time now."

"Sad. Sad. Who else?"

"Lemme see, that's Roger, LeBlanc, Old Man Brown, Sireno's mother, and then Mrs. Castellano's father. That's five, all in one year."

"Gives you the creeps, doesn't it, Mama? Seems like just yesterday when we were going to weddings and wedding showers and baby showers. Remember, Mama? Remember how we used to complain that if the family didn't stop getting married and having babies, we'd all go broke?"

"I remember, but times are different today."

"Look at it this way, Mama. You're what...sixty-eight, sixty-nine?"

"Sixty-eight. Don't make me old."

"All right. You're nearly seventy years old. I'm forty-five. Your generation are aging now, right? And some of your older friends are going, one by one, and you're left. So you think more people are dying. Now when you were my age, your stepmother must have felt the same way?"

"Oh, but not like now. They didn't die much then."

"Don't be silly. Of course, they did. People are dying all the time. How did we ever get on this subject anyway? How's Junior?"

"You didn't hear about your brother? Nobody called and told you?"

"What's he into now?"

"He's got a little sideline business. Selling some kind of lotion or something you wipe on yourself so the mosquitoes won't bite."

"A mosquito repellant?"

"I guess so. The other day he says, 'Mama, don't wait supper for me tonight. I'm going down to South Jersey on a business trip.' So, I says, 'What business trip?' He says, 'I'll tell you about it when I get home.' You know where he went?"

"I'm afraid to ask?"

"A nudist colony."

"Leave it to Junior. If there is a buck to be made, he 'll make it."

"Now all the guys want to go partners with him. Manfred says he'll drive him the next time he goes down. So I said to Junior, 'Didn't you feel ashamed in there?' And he says, 'What for? I keep my eyes straight ahead, just thinking about business. And I say to myself, if anyone says I gotta take off my clothes, I'll just tell them I ain't showing off my ass for no money.'"

"That Junior, Mama! He goes from one thing to another. Still, these little sidelines are better than his sitting around all day watching Super Car, or whatever he's always watching on TV."

"Please. Don't talk."

"Is he still playing poker with the boys?"

"Oh, I made them run last week. Every Friday, they're at the door. They smell when Junior gets paid. But last week, they beeped the horn and Junior was in the bathroom. So I yelled out the door, 'G'wan, you racketeers. Scram! Let my Junior alone.'"

"My God, Mama. What a thing to say. These are pretty rough characters he hangs out with. What did Junior say?"

"Nothing. He better not. I'll throw him out."

"He's thirty-six years old now, Mama, he should be thinking about settling down. I wish he'd meet a nice girl. Boy, this is a toll call. It's going to cost you a fortune. We've been talking a long time, Mama. Is there something bothering you? Is there something you wanted to talk about?"

"Stay up there, Midgie. You're better off, I say."

"We'll see. We'll see. You take care of yourself, now, Mama, and don't worry and if there is anything…"

"Bye, Midgie."

"Bye-bye, Mama."

# Poems

# Lost Playmate

This morning from across the fading field
a blue jay called,

or was it from some other August
of my years?

In the shadow of the cicada's song
I watched
my childhood friend's thin fingers,
delicate as daisy petals,
sew doll clothes.

We dressed and undressed plastic babies
in calico prints,
shared thoughts of future days
in half-grins and giggles,

until Pamela, tired,
leaned back into the afternoon softness
resting her head
against the pear tree.

We listened to a blue jay
then, too,
not knowing
for the last time—
together.

How fragile
the summer green
we touch as children,
dreaming only of instant days.

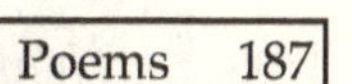

# Sweep Winter Out

This morning I woke early
To sweep winter out of the house
Before the sun had a chance to change its mind.
But when I opened the kitchen door,
A chorus of birds invited me to a concert,
So I sat on the stoop and listened.

# The Gray Morning

The gray morning
Outside my window
Locks in my day.
Inside,
Shadowed rooms
Tease me with familiar faces.
A woodstove in the kitchen burns comfort
And the teakettle whistles a delicate offering.
I put on a record
And curl up in a rocker,
Listen to a guitar
Journey into pain,
But love, too.
Body idle
Adrift in dreams
Chasing grains of sand.

# Lullabye

Esther
in dark rooms
lived her life
with a husband
who raped her daughters.
Her man-child, at sixteen,
from the dark rooms ran
into a morning of sun and green
headed blindly for the Palisades,
stepped off and fell
into a cradle of rocks,
while Esther in dark rooms
bakes sweet, pale sugar cookies.

# A Christmas Memory

Christmas once seasoned slowly—
small things first. A snap in the air,
a word spoken, red-crayoned chimney
on a piece of drawing paper.
Dreaming of a rosy-cheeked doll,
blonde curls, sleepy eyes.
Wistful.

New York and Fourteenth Street—
dark stone fortress of the Salvtion Army.
Street corners where soldiers of the Word
grouped around fire in a coal bucket;
bonnets and bows, lean men singing
salvation and brotherhood.
Thin jingle-jangle of tambourines,
flat wail of coronets
and the swell of a bass drum.

Crowded stores with warm elevators.
Latticed shop windows, glimpses of elves.
Santa Claus and his tinseled helpers
on cold streets. Bargains. Big toys, small toys.
Christmas was counting pennies.

School and Dickens's Scrooge. Gloria
In Excelsis Deo. A box of hard candy.
In the auditorium, a huge fir.
Long cotton stockings, ruffled dresses.
Christmas was make-believe.

Cold winds. Hoping for snow. Sleds.
Buying a tree.
Hanging a wreath on a door;
fake poinsettias in a vase
on a round oak table.
Vermouth and anisette on the buffet
with a tray of wine biscuits for guests.
Papa flushed with holiday spirit,
Mama baking, cleaning, cooking,
Irritable…

Time for stockings to hang
waiting for oranges, nuts,
and always a lump of black coal.
To bed early,
wake with the dawn,
tip-toe down to green boughs,
brilliant balls, and silver glow.
A silent wish,
a single gift,
a catch in the throat.

Christmas was the story
of the birth of a baby boy.
Joyous day!
Sad day!
Quiet when night came.
A day safely tucked away
in a child's memory
a long time ago.

# Punk

She hides in colors black
from head to toe
her young fifteen years.
Look at me, she says,
you can't see me.
I'm invisible.
You can't hurt me.
Find me, she says.

# The Sergeant

The sergeant is coming
to visit.
She's my older sister, Ann,

who guards my memories
on the tip of
her lashing tongue,

turns my fantasies
inside out,

exiles my favorite people
to places where

it 'never happened that way;
you're all wrong."

But, George was there
with her and Henry and me
in the garage that day

we made coffee
in a little toy pot.

It boiled over,
so we drank coffee grounds
from small aluminum cups.

When we played 'wedding,'
Henry married Ann,
and George promised he would
wait for me to grow up.

Then Mama called, loud,
and Ann ran home
when George kissed me.

Why can't she remember
my first love
the way I do?

# On the Passing of the Grandmothers

We greet each other
in a doorway of golden oak.
We stand in rays of sunlight
arcing through tapered pines.
Our arms spiral
round each other
in a large hug.
"Oh, it's so goo-oo-d to see you again.
"It's been too, too long."
Our laughter comforts the pain.
We sit at the polished table
in front of the bay window
where we can watch the narrow stream
pool in circles of opaque stillness.
"I've thought of you so often."
"Are you still reading Krishnamurti?"
We speak of poetry,
the loneliness of being—
the sanity of knowing—
of the wasteland,
T.S. Elliot's, of course.
We remember baby showers, labor pains,
episiotomies and stretch marks,
growing pains.
"I would not like to be a teenager today."
"Could you stand falling in love again?"
We talk of towns and cities
filled with grandchildren
we recognize from snapshots…
TAKEN AT THE BRONX ZOO, AGE 3, 1970
VICKIE, AGE 10. LEAD IN THE CHRISTMAS PAGEANT.
Yellow camomile steams in a teapot.
We sip slowly. Eyes meet over china cups.

We smile. Giggle. Slap each other playfully.
"Where the hell has all the time gone?"
"Do you still like Doc Watson?"
We put on some Lonesome Road.
It feels right.
We're quiet.
We pry.
"And how are you coping since you lost Mike?"
"I still love the banjo."
We tap our feet.
We vow to be there for each other.
In this world, grandmothers are biodegradable.
We share a few tears.
IN MEMORIAM.
The afternoon turns cool.
Only the vague fragrance of camomile
as Doc Watson disappears down Lonesome Road.
We rise reluctantly
and joke about advance reservations
on an ice floe.
Promising, promising to make it a journey for two.

Marie Flaim Tedford, 1985

# Acknowledgements

Over the years some special folks have supported and given counsel on publishing this collection of stories.

Some of these people have passed on, but I want to remember them here: Ron Conte, Margaret Johnson, Leah Wood, Paula Dame, Marge Devlin, Bess Cohen, and Carol Winfield.

I want to say thank you to my husband, Ted. He never gave up, and by now he should be able to recite these stories by heart. He read them, every new draft, over and over.

I'm fortunate to have two daughters, Pat and Paula, also writers, who caught my extra commas, run-on sentences, and other misdemeanors.

Thank you, Pat, for putting it all together, for your patience and expertise.

To friends and members of writing groups over the years, thank you for the honest criticism and "keep going" support: Georgie Lavallee. Eleanor Ott, Susan Stone, Andy Christiansen, Neville Berle, Kathy Harris, Marge Sharpe, and Julie Becker.

And to the writers who perk me up these days on Wednesday mornings, thank you to some special folks with special talents who have kept the "fire" going in my determination to get the book out. Thank you, Mary Elizabeth, Grant Corson, Joe Nelson, and Cynthia Weston.

The League of Vermont Writers has been a gathering of kindred spirits, full of inspiration and opportunity through the years. Thank you for being there.

Thanks to Jonathan Draudt and Harry Crowley for the cover art and design. Harry was just seven years old when he drew Nanny Goat Hill  exactly as I would have suggested.

Thank you, Carolyn Bates of Carolyn Bates Photography, for processing the images of Maria and Annie for the frontice and back cover.

To Mark Pendergrast, Jim DeFilippi, and Dan Close, whose reviews of the book on the back cover made the years of "another draft," and "is it done?" worthwhile, respecting you as writers, I appreciated your comments. Thank you.

Now, I want to include here a thank you to a man who must remain anonymous. He was a reader for a top publishing company who many years ago offered a short course on writing at a college near me. I attended and submitted one of the stories in this collection. At the time, it was the only short story I had worked on, and I knew little about the writing experience. His reaction and comments were more than I ever expected. and I want to say, "Thank you, wherever you are. That was the encouragement I needed to take writing seriously."

# About the Author

Marie Flaim Tedford

Marie Flaim Tedford is an antiquarian book-seller and writer who grew up in New Jersey during the 1920s and '30s. She co-authored *Collectible Books* with her daughter, Pat Goudey O'Brien, for Random House, and wrote the children's book, *The Bearamores Visit the Badlands*, for educational publisher Media Materials. She has written newspaper and magazine articles on books, quilting, crafts, and subjects of local interest. She now lives in Vermont with her family.